"Just what do you want from me?"

"I told you I want the Steller's sea cows."
Jason Merrick stared from Geneva out to the
water. His eyes were as mystically blue as the
seas he inhabited.

"You'll never get them, Jason," she finally said.
"Do you hear me? *Never.*"

"But I will," the mystery man returned coolly.
"You see, I have something *you* want."

Geneva smiled. "Like what? Sunken treasure
ships hidden deep in the Bermuda Triangle?
Riches beyond my wildest dreams? No, the
only thing you have is a vivid imagination."

His mesmerizing gaze returned to her face.
"You're wrong, Geneva," he said with a sexy,
almost mocking smile.

"So what do you have that I want?"

He scrutinized her from head to toe, then
softly said, "Your brother."

Anne Marie Duquette has traveled extensively throughout the United States, first as an air force "brat," then as a member of the military herself. The daughter of a native Colorado wilderness expert and the grand-daughter of a Rocky Mountain miner, she's always been in love with the outdoors. Her books reflect her belief in preserving the land and the sea and the wildlife that inhabit them.

NEPTUNE'S BRIDE

ANNE MARIE DUQUETTE

Silhouette Books

Published by Silhouette Books
America's Publisher of Contemporary Romance

With much gratitude to Save the Manatee Club, Tampa
Electric and Florida Power and Light for their technical
assistance on sirenians, and to Judith Daniels for her
support. Sadly, all extinct or endangered species referred
to in this story actually are extinct or endangered—
including the Steller's sea cow. And my reference to
dolphin therapy with autistics is indeed fact based.

 SILHOUETTE BOOKS

ISBN 0-373-51180-9

NEPTUNE'S BRIDE

Visit Silhouette at www.eHarlequin.com

Printed in U.S.A.

Chapter One

An uncharted island east of Key West...

The dolphins frantically gave the alarm, both their sonar and their frenzied body movements alerting the slumbering man on the beach. Immediately he woke and ran toward the turquoise waters of the sunny lagoon, sending messages of reassurance to the animals he'd sworn to protect.

The moa and dodo birds scattered in fright at their guardian's swift approach, their powerful claws sending up sand. Flocks of rare, exotic parrots took to the afternoon air. Even the prehistoric Archelon sea turtles basking in the shallows hurried out of his way.

The dolphins' agitation increased. The black-and-white colors of the cold-water Commerson dolphins mingled with the familiar gray of the warmer-water bottle-nose in demanding their guardian's presence.

I hear you! the man replied, mentally projecting his response. *I'm coming! I'm coming now!*

His bronze body, naked except for the genital thong that protected him from the island's hot, abrasive sand, knifed through the water. Before he'd even surfaced for his next breath of air, the dolphins had encircled him in a protective fold. He placed both his hands on the dorsal fins offered him and was pulled through the shimmering blue of the lagoon, out toward the deeper ocean depths.

A tumbling avalanche of delphine thoughts assaulted his mind, all of them excited, but none of them distinct.

One at a time! One at a time! the man protested at the onslaught. *I can't understand you all at once!*

Immediately at his command, the chaos in his mind began to subside. Finally, only the dominant male of the bottle-nose school could be heard. The man listened intently.

Are you sure? he asked incredulously, taking in a deep breath when the dolphins surfaced for air. The man closed his mouth tightly as they pulled him back underneath the water and continued their rapid progress out toward open sea.

The Guardian of all Guardians is here—to see me?

An enthusiastic chorus of affirmatives sounded in the man's head. The dolphins pressed their powerful bodies against their protector, the smooth, glossy skins guiding and protecting him.

Their guardian let himself be towed through the tropical waters' warmth with even greater speed. In the five years since he'd exiled himself in this lush marine animal park, he'd learned that no one—not even the former Dr. Jason Merrick—kept the ruler of The Sanctuary waiting.

He closed strong hands even tighter around the dorsal fins at his side and was drawn uneeringly toward the sleek schooner in the distance.

The Senior Guardian was waiting as he surfaced. ''Ahoy, Jase!'' His greeting could barely be heard amidst the chattering squeals of Jase's two schools of dolphins and the high-pitched squeaks of the anchored schooner's escort of porpoises.

Jase nodded acknowledgement and caught the line thrown over to him. With an effortless, hand-over-hand motion, he walked up the port side of the hull and hauled himself onto the deck.

"You called for me?" Jase asked as he coiled the lifeline and stowed it away.

The older man nodded, the action ruffling the flow of his lush white beard. "I did." He studied the younger man with a critical eye.

Suddenly conscious of the other man's flowing robes in contrast to his own bare buttocks, Jase reached for a deck towel, wrapping it around his waist for propriety's sake. He certainly wasn't ashamed of his looks. At age forty he had the body of a much younger man, partially because of the strange preservative qualities of these waters, but mostly because of all the swimming he did in them. His muscles were tight and well defined, and his long, sun-streaked chestnut hair remained free of gray.

Only the haunted look in his eyes gave Jase away. Tragedy marked his true age.

"You're looking well, Jason," the older man said kindly. "You make me feel quite ancient. I am, of course." His ripple of amusement floated over the sea air. "But who likes to be reminded of the passage of years?"

Who, indeed? Jase thought, a shadow clouding his blue eyes. The look vanished just as quickly. "I know how valuable your time is. What can I do for you?"

"Come with me." The Senior Guardian gestured

Jase toward a hand-carved chair on the bow's polished teak deck, then took a seat himself.

"Turn to page three," he ordered.

Jase took the newspaper folded in the older man's hand. The sound of it unfolding was foreign to his ears. He hadn't read a newspaper in the past five years.

"Now read the top story on the left."

Jason did, noticing that the dateline was current: July 12.

Aleutian Islands, Alaska. The discovery of a lone mated pair of arctic Steller's sea cows has been announced by marine biologist Dr. Geneva Kelsey of the Florida Sirenian Institute.

"But this can't be! They're extinct!" Jase immediately exclaimed.

"So we all thought. Keep reading."

According to Dr. Kelsey, a specialist in sirenians (manatees/dugongs), the Steller's sea cow was discovered in 1741 in Alaska and supposedly slaughtered to extinction by 1768. Her photographs—

Jase tore his eyes away from the article. "Photographs? She took *photographs?*" He scanned the newspaper page, then zipped through the other pages in the section, but there were no related photographs anywhere, not of the sea cows, nor of the woman.

"It was a late-breaking story. There will be no photos until tomorrow," the Senior Guardian said. "However, I do have these."

He passed over a folder filled with glossy black and

whites. Jase immediately went through them one by one, staring at the gray heads, the massive, twenty-six-foot-long bodies, the split tail flukes, the short, stubby pectoral limbs.

"Where did you get these?" Jase came to the end of the pile and flipped through them again more slowly, unable to believe his eyes. "Are they authentic?"

The older man smiled. "They certainly are," he said, ignoring Jase's first question and only answering the second.

"If this is true—"

"It is."

"Then we *must* have these animals." Jase quickly scanned the rest of the article.

Marine parks worldwide are clamoring for possession of these rare mammals, but Dr. Kelsey is cautious. "Information on this species is sketchy at best, even to those specialists such as myself. In addition, other surviving sirenian species are warm-water dwellers, as are their man-made holding facilities. I won't reveal the location of these arctic animals and decide their future without careful consideration. The fate of such a priceless discovery can't possibly be reached overnight."

"Damn! They don't have much about her background." He folded up the newspaper with disgust and passed it back to the Senior Guardian.

"I have everything you need to know," the older man replied. "Including this."

He handed Jase one last photograph, a photograph kept separate from the others.

Jase looked at it, his breath catching in his throat. It was a full-color shot of a woman—but not just any ordinary woman. The subject in the picture was extraordinarily beautiful. The swimsuit-clad body was undeniably feminine: the legs long, the waist trim, with luxurious, yet not overwhelming, curves. But it was her face that grabbed Jase's interest. Framed in waist-length ebony hair and thick bangs, it was full of life. The brown eyes twinkled, and the lush, full lips were parted in laughter. Whoever had taken the photograph had captured not only the woman's figure—they'd captured her spirit, too.

For the first time in five years Jase found himself wondering about a woman…*this* woman. There was something about her photograph, something more than just her physical appearance, that intrigued him. For the first time in ages Jase felt a stirring in his loins. The sensation took him truly by surprise. He'd been alone for so very, very long.…

Jase returned the photograph and strove to keep his voice devoid of interest. "You said you had more on her than just a picture?" he asked, strangely eager to learn more.

"I do. You will have plenty of time to review the information on Dr. Kelsey before you leave."

Jase froze. "You're sending *me* to get these sea cows?"

"Correct, my friend."

Jase shook his head, confused. "But why not send one of the other guardians? My doctorate's in psychology. I'm no marine biologist."

"You know just as much, if not more, about marine life, than any of my other guardians, Jase."

Jase shrugged. "As I have no contact with them, I couldn't say."

The old man's eyes narrowed in a sudden burst of irritation. "Only because you refuse the company of others. You refuse to use your boat, and refuse to let other boats into your lagoon. It is unhealthy for *any* creature to avoid his own kind for so long. You have no friends. You have no mate. Yet there are many here, men and women alike, who would welcome your presence in their lives."

Jase was defiantly silent, and the old man's annoyance faded as quickly as it had appeared.

"Forgive me, son. I digress."

"The sea cows should be our first priority right now," Jase replied stiffly.

The old man paused, then said, "You and the sea cows are *both* a priority, Jase."

Jase's eyes narrowed cautiously. "How so?"

"Depending on a man's intelligence and personality, this aquatic preserve gives different powers to different people. Most guardians can only communicate with one marine species. A rare handful can speak to a few species. But only two men in this sanctuary can speak to *all* the marine life. I am one of them. You are the other."

Jase lifted his chin in acknowledgement.

"In the five short years you have lived with us, you have quickly learned our secrets, Jase. *All* of them."

"I'd never betray this place," Jase replied quietly.

The older man waved his hand in the air, dismissing the younger man's words. "That was never in doubt. However, you have great powers—powers that will be needed to navigate the dangerous waters of the arctic, powers that will allow you to speak to these precious rarities, powers that will safely bring the Steller's sea cows home to us.''

Jase frowned. As intriguing, as beautiful, as the woman in the photograph was, she was part of the world he'd deliberately left behind. He hated the thought of leaving his peaceful island and his familiar sea wards. His two schools of dolphins felt his pain and sent back warm comfort. Jase wished he was back in the water with them but didn't act on that thought. Neither did he readily give in to the man seated before him.

''Like you, I can only talk to species I've first made direct contact with,'' Jase reminded him. ''As we all thought the Steller's sea cows were extinct, no guardian has any advantage over any other. It doesn't matter *who* you send for the initial meeting. Once you learn the secret of their location from Geneva Kelsey, anyone will do. It doesn't have to be me.''

''But it does, Jase. Next to me, you have the best chance of success with them. And I am needed here.''

Jase found himself staring at the photograph of Geneva Kelsey in the other man's hand, then forced himself to look away. ''You know my feelings on this subject. I'm happy here. I wasn't in the real world. I don't want to go back!''

The older man sighed. ''The situation leaves me no choice. You and I both know these sea cows will not survive in captivity. For such a rare prize, I would send only the very best of my guardians. *You* are my best, Jase. I must insist.''

His lips compressed in a tight line. Jase knew the die was cast, but not because of the older man's authority. It was the picture of the woman that had finally caused him to relent.

"Very well. I'll do as you ask." Then, annoyed at the older man's triumphant look, he added curtly, "But you know I need to be in direct contact with the sea cows for my first mental contact. I can't bring them back here if I don't know where they are! What makes you think this woman is going to give a stranger her sea cows?"

"Because, my friend, we have something she wants."

"Wanting isn't the same as *having*. We can't bribe her with our marine specimens." Jase stood up and paced the deck, ignoring the towel that fell to the ground. "We both know the rules here. No marine life in The Sanctuary is ever allowed to leave."

"Nor are any *trespassers*."

Jase instantly picked up on the emphasized word. "Dr. Kelsey has a relative trapped here in The Sanctuary?"

"Correct."

"Who?"

"The Survivor."

Jase's eyes opened wide. The Survivor had come to them as a fifteen-year-old boy. Now he was a mature, twenty-year veteran of The Sanctuary. No one in the history of The Sanctuary had ever lived so long in its confines without joining the ranks of creature caretakers known as Guardians. Although trespassers to The Sanctuary, both marine and human alike, were never allowed to leave, The Sanctuary treated all its inhabitants kindly, especially its human wards. Sooner or later those humans willingly, even happily, swore loyalty to The Sanctuary and the wards in its keeping and became active participants in The Sanctuary's society. There were no exceptions ever recorded, except for The Survivor.

Not only had The Survivor refused to take the pledge of loyalty, he'd defiantly refused to divulge even his name. As both his parents had died instantly in the plane crash that brought their son to The Sanctuary, he'd been given the nickname The Survivor.

"So, our unpledged ward now has a name," Jase said with wonder.

"Yes. He is Thomas Kelsey, Geneva's twin brother."

"Twins?"

The old man smiled. "Most fortuitous for us. In this matter, the Fates have been kind."

Jase shook his head in amazement. In his exile here, Thomas Kelsey had been the only other human Jase encountered on a regular basis, for their islands were in close proximity, and they shared the same fishing grounds. Thomas was no trouble. In fact, he was extremely self-sufficient, although unlike Jase, he preferred the company of others. Jase and The Survivor exchanged civil nods from time to time—but he hadn't known the man's name. Now he knew even that.

"Thomas and Geneva Kelsey..." Jase's voice trailed off in amazement. Suddenly he wondered if the sister was as stubborn, as determined, as self-sufficient, as the brother. In fact, he found himself wondering a lot of things about Geneva Kelsey.

Perhaps, just perhaps, this trip wouldn't be such an unpleasant chore, after all. Jase smiled at the thought. It was a rare display for him, and the expression didn't reach his eyes, but it was a smile just the same.

He looked up to see his superior watching him

closely. "Be very careful, my friend. Use the information wisely."

"Oh, I will." Jase's smile grew. "I most certainly will."

He climbed up on the railing of the rocking schooner and straightened, his bronze body magnificently balanced against the powerful ocean swells. At his command, the waiting dolphins instantly scattered, leaving the water beneath him free for his dive. But first Jase spoke his final words to the Senior Guardian.

"The Steller's sea cows will be ours. One way or another, Geneva Kelsey *will* reveal her secret to me."

"DR. KELSEY! DR. KELSEY!"

Geneva Kelsey looked out her Jacksonville office window and frowned. She didn't see the beauty of the St. Johns River, home of Florida's freshwater manatees. She didn't even notice the beautifully manicured grounds of the Florida Sirenian Institute. All she saw were the hordes of reporters waiting outside, hordes pounding on her window because they couldn't get inside past security, hordes standing between her and the parking lot.

If only there'd been some other way she could have proven her claim without publishing those photographs! But no one in their right mind, whether a member of the public or the scientific world, would have believed that a species supposedly extinct for two centuries had resurfaced. And Geneva *desperately* needed to keep her credibility—and fund-raising abilities—intact if she was to help those Steller's sea cows.

Unfortunately, the best credibility in the world wasn't going to get her to the car. Neither was cowering here in her office waiting for them to go away. It would be a long wait. Security had been called away to an attempted break-in down at the labs.

"Damn!" Geneva pushed at her black bangs and sighed.

Someone banged on her window. "Dr. Kelsey, talk to us!"

It was quite obvious the mob wasn't going anywhere. Geneva lifted her chin, grabbed her briefcase and headed for the parking lot.

The mob converged immediately as Geneva stepped outside into the humidity of a Florida summer. Cameras whirred, video rolled and microphones were shoved in her face.

"Dr. Kelsey, have you decided to reveal the location of the Steller's sea cows yet?"

"No, I haven't. As I've repeatedly told you, the safest place for these animals right now is in their native habitat." Geneva descended the steps of the institute, her hand on the railing to brace herself against the crowd.

"But how will you find them again? Alaska is a big place. Even an Eskimo like yourself will have a hard time searching all the ocean."

Geneva stopped in her tracks, her brown eyes flashing. "First of all, the correct term for my mother's people is Inuit, not Eskimo. Secondly, my father's family is native Floridian. They can trace their ancestry back to old Spain. If you *must* label me, please use the term 'sirenian specialist' or 'marine biologist.' When it comes to finding the sea cows again, my knowledge of sirenian behavior will be the primary factor—*not* my genetic makeup."

There was a sudden awkward silence broken by a

voice in the back of the crowd. "You might want to add that the name Eskimo was originally applied to the Inuit by the Algonquin Indians, and means 'he eats it raw.' A little education never hurts, especially when it comes to the press."

Geneva looked up in amazement, searching the crowd for the owner of the male voice. Very few people knew that particular fact. And those few who did certainly weren't from Florida. "Who said that?" she demanded.

"I did." Geneva saw a ripple of motion in the crowd as a tall body passed through. The pressing throng of media that had harassed her immediately parted for him.

"You're not press," she observed, taking in the brilliant blue eyes, the sun-darkened, bronze skin, and the broad, muscular shoulders and arms. He was a man of the sun—a man of the sea. She'd bet her life on it. The others around her paled in significance as she studied him. A strange excitement, a sensation of anticipation, flooded through her.

"Are you a colleague?"

"Of sorts." His lips turned upward ever so slightly. "I'm here to help you with your Steller's sea cows, Geneva Kelsey. If you'll let me."

Geneva was bumped by another impatient media person. "Lord knows I could use some help, Mr.—"

"Call me Jase."

She nodded. The Sunbelt was famous for its informality. Cultivated manners and precise etiquette disappeared along with shoes, coats and chilly inhibitions in the Florida sun.

"Jase, I'd be happy to talk to you, but we've got to get away from this mob." Geneva scowled at the reporters. "I've answered the same questions for these people the past three days, but they refuse to leave me alone."

A flicker of emotion crossed Jase's face. "Eventually, they will. Even the most sensational stories inevitably die."

Geneva paused, but before she could wonder about the odd tone to his voice, she felt him take her briefcase from her, then sling his free arm around her waist. Within minutes he'd cleared a path through the crowd, discouraged them from following with a few sharp words and had her making good progress toward the parking lot.

"Thanks," Geneva said, sighing with real relief as they approached her car. "I don't know how we got away from them so easily, but I appreciate it. You'll have to let me in on your secret."

The man smiled. "All you need is another six inches and some bulk."

Geneva grimaced. "Brute strength is *not* my strong point, I know. But this body and I do okay in the water."

There was no sultry, come-on male response such as "You certainly do," or a leering "I can see that."

Instead, Jase was silent. But his eyes left her face to give her a slow, assessing look. She watched as he took in every inch of her, top to bottom. First he noted her long black hair worn in a French braid, then studied her delicate facial features—Alaskan Inuit dominated by the aristocratic Spanish ancestry of Florida's early settlers.

His eyes lingered over the lush curves that her finely conditioned swimmer's body couldn't quite disguise. Then his gaze returned to her face. Instead of feeling insulted or embarrassed, Geneva allowed Jase his boldness. Fair was fair. She'd been doing some assessing herself. Her scientist's mind had noted the perfect symmetry of his proportions, while her woman's body had felt a jolt of pure sexual attraction.

There was no doubt about it. As a strictly physical specimen, he was magnificent. But as for his character, that was still an unknown, which meant she should be cautious.

There was a quiet pause, then Jase spoke. "You're a very beautiful woman. Your pictures don't do you justice."

Geneva was secretly flattered, but her reserved nature didn't permit her to show outright capitulation. "Newspaper photos rarely do," she said lightly. "You never told me your last name, Jase." She started to unlock her car door, but Jase firmly took the keys and did it himself.

"Guardian. Jase Guardian." At her raised eyebrows, he added with a wry twist of his lips, "It's an unusual name, but I can assure you it's quite legitimate."

Geneva nodded and allowed him to open her door. "Do you have a title, Jase? A doctorate, perhaps?"

"I prefer not to use it" was his curt response. He handed Geneva her briefcase, then strode around to the passenger side, unlocked that door, slid in and gave her back the keys. "Can we drive somewhere quiet?" he said at her surprised look. "I'd like to talk to you in private, away from these news hounds."

After a moment's hesitation, Geneva started the car. "There's an old pier down the road a ways. It's usually deserted this time of day. I like to eat my lunch there," she explained.

Jase nodded his agreement.

"What about your car?" Geneva asked curiously.

"My driver's license has expired. I took a cab here."

"I see." She felt a twinge of uneasiness. After all, this man was a stranger, yet she'd consented to drive to an abandoned location with him.

"I just want to talk with you. Nothing else. I won't harm you, Geneva Kelsey."

His voice startled her. Had her apprehension been that obvious? Suddenly she felt very foolish. "Sorry," she said as she pulled out of the parking lot and headed toward the little-used side road that would take them to the pier. "What with all the publicity lately, I'm very jumpy. And more than a little wary."

Jase turned in his seat so he was facing her. "You have good reason to be. You've discovered treasure, Geneva. Men kill for treasure."

Geneva didn't like the way his words caused the hair on the back of her neck to prickle. But he was right, she thought during the short drive. She did have treasure. The Steller's sea cows had been discovered by the Russians in 1741 during the fur trade. The saltwater dwellers made good eating and became a staple diet of the Russian ships. Unfortunately the sea cows had never been a prolific race, and their small numbers were gone a short twenty-seven years later.

Or so they'd thought, until one Geneva Kelsey on vacation in Alaska had spotted a lone pair. The idea of her sea cows being fought over frightened her. Certainly the unscrupulous could profit from her discovery. The Steller's sea cows would be worth a fortune alive *or* dead to any serious collector.

It wasn't until Geneva pulled up at the deserted pier

overlooking the St. Johns River that she bluntly asked, "And you, Jase Guardian?" She shut off the ignition and gave him her full attention. "Are you after my treasure, too?"

Jase didn't answer. He climbed out of the car, opened up her door for her, then reached in with one strong hand.

"What are you doing?" The bad feeling Geneva had when he didn't immediately answer her question increased when he deftly pocketed her keys.

"Keeping you from changing your mind." He gently eased her out of the car, then slammed the door behind her. "If it's safe, let's walk to the end of the pier."

"It's safe." *But are you?*

"Yes, I'm safe, too." He answered her unspoken question, watched her react, then gave her a mocking glance. "Don't ever play poker, Geneva. Your face is quite readable." As they reached the pier and stepped up on it, he withdrew her car keys. "Here. Will these make you feel better?"

Geneva took the keys and shoved them in the pocket of her slacks. "A little. Now, what is it you want, Mr. Guardian?"

"I see I've fallen out of grace, *Dr. Kelsey.*" His voice carried no hint of anger, only calm acceptance. "No matter. I'm here for one reason only. Or rather two," he corrected himself significantly.

"You want my sea cows." Geneva was furious. And beneath that fury was an odd feeling of betrayal and pain. "And I thought you were different. You're just like every other vulture I've met since I published those photographs."

She tried to sweep past him, to get back to the car,

but he deliberately blocked her way. "Move it, mister."

"I want you to listen to me carefully, Geneva. I know just as much about sirenians as you do, if not more. Those sea cows won't survive in captivity, and they don't stand a snowball's chance in hell in Alaska now that everyone's looking for them. I have a place where they'll be safe, where they can breed and prosper."

"Just where do you propose to put them, Mr. Guardian? In your bathtub?"

"There's no need for sarcasm. There *is* a safe sanctuary in the wild for them. I want to take them there."

"Right. You're just a concerned conservationist looking out for the sea cows' welfare."

Jase took a deliberate step closer toward her. Geneva refused to be intimidated. She turned her back on him, looking over the end of the pier at the murky waters of the St. Johns.

"Turn around, Dr. Kelsey." His voice was quiet, but there was an iron determination, a ring of authority in it that Geneva couldn't ignore. She turned around.

"I'd like to tell you about The Sanctuary. For the sea cows' sake, ask as many questions as you want. I'll try to answer every one of them as best I can."

"All right." Geneva defiantly crossed her arms against her chest. "For starters, you can tell me where this so-called safe sanctuary is. And *then* you can tell me where you're from."

A strange, unreadable expression flickered in Jase's eyes. Despite herself, Geneva realized she was holding her breath.

"Both my home and The Sanctuary are found in the same place, Geneva. I'm from the Bermuda Triangle."

Chapter Two

"The *Bermuda Triangle?*" Geneva couldn't believe her ears. She didn't know whether to laugh aloud at the sheer nonsense of the idea, or to scream with frustration. She decided on the latter.

"You dragged me out here to listen to fairy tales about haunted oceans? Next you'll be telling me you live aboard the *Flying Dutchman* and Moby Dick is your mascot!"

"I know it's a difficult concept to grasp."

He actually seemed amused by her tirade! "Difficult! It's ridiculous! Do you really expect me to believe you?"

"Not at first. But you will...eventually."

Geneva took one look at the ominous intensity in his blue eyes and forced herself to stay calm. She might not believe in this nonsense, but the man before her did. And he was standing at the shore end of the pier between her and her car.

"Look, Mr. Guardian—if that really *is* your name," she couldn't help adding. "Even if I bought all this, the Steller's sea cows are *arctic* animals. The waters of the Bermuda Triangle are *tropical*. The sea cows would still die."

"No. There are many different environments within The Sanctuary, many different conditions that you wouldn't expect in tropical waters. But they do exist, because we *make* them exist."

Geneva felt a shiver go down her spine. *Dear God, I'm trapped on a pier with a crazy man. How am I going to get out of this one?*

"Who's this *us?*" she asked in a carefully neutral voice. *Keep him talking. That's what all the books say.*

"We call ourselves guardians. I and others like myself have sworn to protect The Sanctuary and the creatures within. That includes marine life long thought extinct. We even have rare animals on our islands, although land space is very limited." Geneva saw his eyes fire with passion. "It's a marine biologist's dream, Geneva. Your sea cows would be safe. They could breed there, thrive there, without the threat of man."

Geneva swallowed hard. "This is all very interesting," she said in a hoarse voice. She refrained from glancing at her car, but she did slide her hand into her pocket for the reassuring feel of her car keys. If she could just get him off the pier, she'd have a chance to make a mad dash out of here.

"Why don't we go back to the institute? I'm certain my colleagues would be very interested in what you have to say."

Geneva saw the enthusiasm in his eyes turn to disappointment. However, his voice remained level, even friendly.

"I was hoping we could do this the easy way, but—" He sighed heavily. "Give me the car keys, Geneva." He held out his hand, palm up.

Geneva lifted her chin. "No."

Jase took a few steps closer, causing Geneva to retreat even nearer to the end of the pier.

Why had she ever agreed to come to such a deserted place with a crazed man? She could scream her head off and no one would hear!

"If you don't, I'll have to take them from you. Either way, the end result will be the same."

She reached into her pocket, yanked out the keys and defiantly hurled them with all her strength out over the river.

Jase followed the arc of descent until the keys sank with a little splash. This time when she met his eyes again she knew she'd angered him. But still, his voice was calm.

"That was very foolish. Do I look like your run-of-the-mill car thief?"

"Are you?" she countered.

"No. I *am* trying to be patient, because I know how farfetched this all sounds. Before I accidentally found my way to The Sanctuary—what you call the Bermuda Triangle—I wouldn't have believed it myself."

"Holding me hostage on a pier certainly won't convince me, either!" Geneva flung back.

"I'm not stopping you from leaving," Jase replied. "You could have left any time for any place, even a public place—with me in tow, of course. That is, until you threw your car keys into the river." He laughed softly at her stricken expression. "Really, Geneva, what *were* you thinking?" He took still another step closer.

Geneva turned around. There were a few scant feet between her and the river. Could she possibly outswim him? It might be worth a try. Her low-heeled pumps would kick off easily. She unobtrusively slipped one shoe off.

"You might as well take off the rest of your clothes, too," he calmly announced. "No sense getting them soaked if you want to swim."

Geneva stood awkwardly in one stocking-clad foot and one pump. "Isn't that what you were planning?" he said reasonably. Geneva watched in shock as he started unbuttoning his own shirt. "Actually, a swim is exactly what I'd hoped for."

"A swim?" she echoed.

"Yes. So I can prove to you that I am what I say." He went on, button after button. "Go on, Geneva. Take off your clothes."

"I—" What was it the talk shows said on how not to be a victim? She wasn't sure, but she certainly knew what it was her aunt had always said! Don't pick up strangers!

Damn it, Geneva! How could you have been so stupid?

"If that's what you want," she replied in a firm voice, stepping out of her other pump. *I'll get undressed, but only so I can swim like hell when I jump off this pier!* She wasn't a marine biologist for nothing. She swam laps, she swam with her manatees, she snorkeled, she scuba dived. And right now, she had enough adrenaline shooting through her veins to outswim Mark Spitz himself.

Slowly she unbuttoned her blouse. First the top button at the collar, then the next, until the top of the two-piece swimsuit she always wore under her clothes to work was exposed. Her fingers froze halfway down as she saw him carelessly toss his shirt onto the splintered old wood of the pier. Geneva stared at the blatant strength in those broad shoulders and well-defined pectoral muscles. Her heart sank. She'd never escape once those sinewy arms were around her. Well, she'd just make certain he never touched her.

Jase slipped his feet out of his leather Dock-sides, then unzipped his jeans. Geneva stared, her breath coming in ragged gasps. When he caught her looking, she concentrated on removing her shirt and dropping it on the dock. Aware of his every movement, she unzipped her slacks and slipped out of them, her nylon anklets catching and running on the pier's rough wood.

She looked up again and saw that Jase was watching her intently. She also saw that he was now totally undressed except for a minuscule bit of covering, with no tan lines visible anywhere. Under any other circumstances, at any other time, she would have enjoyed studying the muscled thighs, the tautness of the deeply tanned abdomen, the proud male outline under that scanty thong.

This was *not* one of those times.

Geneva forced her eyes away from his bronze body and pulled off her snagged nylons with a jerky motion. Her eyes scanned the water, trying to gauge the river current and marine traffic. Maybe she could reach safety by swimming to the nearest boater. There was one far off in the distance, but she was a strong swimmer. She would be able to make it, but only if she could outdistance him.

"You ought to take off the bikini top, Geneva. It'll just soak your blouse when we get dressed again."

Geneva's head swiveled back toward him. "You're going to let me get dressed again?" she asked incredulously.

"Of course I am!" For the first time she saw evidence of his temper. "I'm no mad rapist, Dr. Kelsey. I have no intention of hiding any woman's violated body in the river. I won't hurt you. You have my word."

"Right." Geneva didn't bother hiding her sarcasm. "I'm supposed to trust a man who claims he's from the Bermuda Triangle?"

"For heaven's sake, use your head, Geneva! Even if I *were* deranged, I'd still want your sea cows! Would I hurt the only person in the world who knows where they are?"

"I—I don't know. Would you?" she demanded.

"No," he said angrily. "We're wasting time. I've tried to be patient, but obviously you're not going to believe me until I prove it to you. Get in the water, Geneva. *Now.*"

"Wait!" Geneva took a deep breath. She needed a diversion if she wanted to get a good head start on him. "Let me take my top off first, like you suggested."

When he didn't protest, she reached around behind her back, pretending to search for the hook for the bikini top. She saw his gaze drop from her face to the full, lush curves of her still-covered breasts. *He can't wait to get an eyeful,* Geneva realized with satisfaction. In the split second that he was distracted, she made her move.

She whirled and launched herself forward in a racing dive that drove her far along the surface of the water. Then she was swimming as if her life depended on it....

She'd only taken two breaths when she heard the sound of a second body entering the water. Geneva dived deep, hoping to lose her pursuer in the murky waters. If she couldn't reach the boat, perhaps she could backtrack toward the shore while he was still searching for her, then hide in the lush trees lining the river's edge.

Why, oh why, had she thrown away her car keys?

Geneva rose for breath—and found herself chest to chest with her waiting pursuer. She pushed against him, struggled with all her might, but couldn't escape. He pulled her hard against his chest and took her down deep into the water again. The more she struggled, the tighter he held her. Forcing herself not to panic, she relaxed, and the iron grip relaxed, too. But they were still far below the surface.

Dear God, I'm going to die, she thought as the oxygen supply in her bloodstream ran out bit by bit. Her chest and throat burned with painful need. She needed to breathe! The clenched fingers that had punched and scratched her assailant opened and reached for his face. With two frantic hands she tapped his nose and mouth in silent supplication, begging him, pleading with him, to help her.

Immediately his powerful legs kicked them upward. He lifted Geneva in his arms. Her head broke the surface first. She sucked in air, the cutting freshness of it almost as painful as the stale air held so long in her chest. Despite the pain, she eagerly gulped in more.

"Put your arms around my neck," he ordered.

Geneva needed no urging, for her trembling muscles were weak and oxygen-starved. She threw her arms around him and held him tightly. Immediately, her captor released her waist and began treading water for both of them. Only that and her hold around his neck prevented her slipping back into the weed-choked depths of the St. Johns. She closed her eyes, trying to still her shaking limbs.

One of Jase's arms stopped treading water and reached for her. He gently pushed her head down on his shoulder, then stroked her wet hair with soothing strokes. Geneva felt some of her trembling subside and wondered if it was the oxygen reentering her body, or his touch. Suddenly she was aware of *his* body—his legs tangled with hers beneath the water, his hard chest pressed against hers and flattening her soft breasts. Geneva felt her pulse quicken, and this time it wasn't just fear that motivated her increased heartbeat.

It was passion....

With that realization, she immediately lifted her head from his shoulder. Danger as an aphrodisiac belonged only in the movies...and this wasn't the movies. She couldn't afford to let his chemistry—or her treacherous body's attraction to him—distract her. Geneva turned her head, not toward him, but toward her car on shore.

"Look at me, Geneva."

She lifted a face streaming with river water to his.

"Are you all right?" he asked quietly, his hand still gently cradling the base of her neck, his fingers threaded through her hair.

Geneva nodded.

"You won't try to get away again, will you?"

She shook her head. At least, not right this second. She'd wait until she had a better chance at it.

The talk shows haven't been much help, she thought, a measure of calm returning. *They've never said how not to be a victim when forcibly held under water. Maybe she'd write a letter to Oprah—if she ever got out of this mess....*

"I promised I wouldn't hurt you, and I won't. But I can't release you until you hear what I have to say. Will you listen, Geneva?"

"It appears I don't have much of a choice." Her reply was quick, her anger coming through loud and clear.

For a moment, she caught a grudging look of admiration in his eyes. His hand left her hair to stroke her cheek. "That's the spirit, my Sweet Survivor."

Geneva jerked her head away at his touch, her hands flying off his corded neck. But he was quicker. Immediately his hands were hard on her waist and they started to sink. Geneva knew better than to physically avoid him again until she regained her strength once more. Grimacing, she put her hands back around his neck so he could tread water once more.

He nodded his approval and said, "It appears courage runs in your family."

"You don't know me! And you certainly don't know my family! Do whatever it is you have to do, then let me go!"

"I see you have your breath back," Jase said with satisfaction. "We're going for a swim, you and I. I want us side by side, near arms around each other's waists, far arms hand in hand. When you have to breathe, squeeze my hand and I'll surface. I want to spend as much time underwater as possible."

"In the St. Johns? The water is murky and full of vegetation! Visibility is barely ten feet!"

"For you, perhaps," he said with a strange smile. He positioned her at his side. First he took her near hand and placed it around his waist. Then he grasped her far hand and held it against the washboard muscles of his stomach. His powerful leg kicks still kept them both afloat. "Tell me, Geneva, how many manatees do you usually find around this pier?"

"At one time? Not many..." Geneva tossed her head, trying to throw back the long wet hair from her face. The dressy French braid had disappeared sometime during her struggles. "Manatees usually share the same feeding grounds, but they aren't a true herding society." She refused to tread water with him, conserving her breath so she could talk, and her strength so she could escape. "Unless a mother is with her calf, or a female is in estrous with pursuing males, they're only semisocial this time of year."

Jase's strange smile still remained. "I think we'll start out with five manatees."

"*Five—*"

"Then ten manatees. Then if we're very lucky, fifteen. Such easy numbers to work with, don't you think?"

"Jase, these creatures are endangered! Do you know what that means? You won't find fifteen! We'll be lucky to see *one!*"

"Ah, but you're with *me* now."

"What difference does that make?"

"I can talk to them," he announced. "I can call them from miles away. I told them I was here yesterday and reminded them again today. They're waiting, Geneva, even as we speak."

At his odd words, Geneva found some of her courage start to fail again. *Dear God, she was trapped in the water with a man who thought he was Dr. Doolittle! She might as well dig her own grave. No way in hell was she getting out of this alive.* Something in her face must have alerted him, for he leaned over and kissed her cheek.

"I promised not to hurt you, remember?"

"Please, Jase, let me go. I'll get dressed and hitch a ride back to the institute. I won't say a word about all this, I swear."

"I can't let you go, Geneva. Not yet." He kissed her again, this time on the corner of her eye. "Don't look like that. I'll keep you safe."

Her eyes were wide with alarm. But despite her fear, Geneva couldn't help but notice the ring of sincerity in his voice.

"You won't do anything crazy?" she asked, hating the frightened catch in her voice, hating him hearing it even more.

"No. Now take a deep breath and nod when you're ready to go down. I won't dive until you give me the signal."

Geneva closed her eyes and prayed like she'd never prayed before. When she opened them, Jase was still there, his body holding hers fast. *So much for trying the religious approach,* she thought caustically.

She tried one last clever lie. "I have scuba gear in the trunk of my car—gear for two. Couldn't we go get it first?"

"You know as well as I do that escaping air from scuba gear frightens manatees, Dr. Kelsey. Scuba divers can't get close to them. Only snorkelers or free-swimming divers like us do."

Geneva bit her lip. Damn him! He might be a nut case, but he knew something about manatees, after all. There was nothing to do but take in a deep breath, nod...and dive.

It wasn't as bad as she had expected, Geneva thought to herself. At least the sun was out. Visibility was a good fifteen feet instead of the ten she'd anticipated. The pier pilings were an excellent reference point—as long as they stuck close to the relatively shallow water near them. There was no way Geneva wanted to go out near the swifter, deeper section of the St. Johns and its boat traffic.

She carefully conserved her air, letting Jase do the bulk of the swimming, and praying like mad that he would surface when she squeezed his hand. *If he didn't...* Geneva was just about to test his promise when Jase abruptly stopped. He changed from a prone position in the water to an upright position, still keeping her tight against his side and pointed with the hand that held hers.

Geneva blinked. *Manatees!*

A pair of sirenians closed in, their rounded bodies graceful in the water. Geneva stared at a young mother and her calf as they slowly hovered in the depth. Then another mother and calf, the baby much younger than the first one, floated by. Geneva's eyes were wide open. She watched as a massive male approached, his back gouged and marred by old propeller scars from the boats that were the freshwater dwellers' enemies.

Geneva was spellbound. Vibrant sirenian life was all around her—before her, above her, below her. She was aware of the circling manatees, aware of Jase encircling her with his arm, aware of her own amazement. Aware of her air giving out...

Reluctantly she squeezed Jase's hand, letting him propel her toward the surface.

Her eyes sparkled with delight. Jase held her by the waist as she caught her breath again. "You did count five, didn't you?"

"Let's go back!" she begged. She missed the look of satisfaction in his eyes as she took in a deep breath.

Only this time was different. She didn't flinch from his touch. This time she let him take her back under the water. All thoughts of escape vanished. Geneva was a willing, eager participant.

Fascinated, she watched as more manatees appeared. They joined the others hovering gracefully in the murky waters, their stubby pectorals and rounded tails gently directing their bodies. The nursing mothers began to feed on the rich growth around the pier, their flexible lips delicately pulling plants into their mouths. One calf attached himself to one of the mother's two armpit nipples.

Geneva longed for her underwater camera, wished for her face mask for better clarity, wished the moment would never end. She'd seen manatees before, but never like this. Despite their thirteen-foot size, they were usually shy, retiring creatures she observed from a distance. Geneva watched in fascination until the constraints of her body forced her again to give Jase the signal for air.

"That was ten," he said back on the surface, his eyes mirroring her pleasure. "Ready for more?"

"Oh, yes!" This time she would have swum down herself alone, but Jase was still at her side, his arm around her waist, her hand in his. Now the water around the pier was *full* of manatees. Geneva picked out a few pregnant females, their gestating bodies twice Jase's length and bulkier than the males.

One young female actually came up and nuzzled her. Geneva was delighted but kept her hands in contact with Jase at all times. She knew manatees in general liked body contact with both living and inanimate objects, but she'd trained herself not to interfere with them in the wild. They could touch you, but you weren't allowed to initiate the contact. "Handling" the rare manatee was illegal in Florida. Interfering with their normal behavior was strictly forbidden.

Yet the sensation of swimming with the manatees— so very, very many of them!—was indescribable. It didn't compare to swimming with the creatures in the institute's rehabilitation tanks. Nothing could. Geneva wouldn't have missed this experience for the world. Despite the terror this strange man had subjected her to, she was grateful. Unwilling to leave, she forced herself to concentrate on holding her breath a few seconds longer.

This time it was Jase who initiated the swim to the surface, not Geneva. He held her tightly as she gasped for air, then choked and sputtered on a splash of water in her haste to breathe. Jase turned on his side and locked her against his chest, then towed her to the shore with powerful strokes. Once near the riverbank, he carried her out and gently set her down in the soft sand.

"That was very foolish, Geneva. You should have squeezed my hand," Jase said quietly. "Don't you realize you're as valuable as the sea cows?"

Geneva couldn't answer. She could only stare at him with wide eyes, and breathe. After only a few minutes of rest, Geneva stood up again. "Let's go back in the water," she said breathlessly.

"No." Jase stood up himself to take her arm and hold her back. "You're tired."

"I'm fine!" Forgotten were her fears of earlier. To see a herd of endangered manatees right at her fingertips was nothing short of miraculous! "I didn't see if any had fresh injuries. The boat traffic in this river is deadly to manatees! If there're any recent propeller gashes on them, I need to get my rescue and rehab people out here and—''

''The manatees are all healthy. They're also gone.'' He reached for her chin with his free hand and turned her face toward him. ''I sent them back to their original locations.''

''You sent them—'' Geneva took in a deep, frustrated gulp of air and shook her chin free of his grasp. Sometime during their dives she'd lost her fear of him. That didn't mean she trusted the poor, misguided fool, but somehow she instinctively knew he wouldn't hurt her if she disagreed.

''Listen to me, Jase. You no more sent those manatees away than you called them.''

''Then how do you explain this herd?''

Geneva bit her lip and said nothing.

''This wasn't a mating herd of males after an eligible female, Geneva. And it's not time for herds to congregate at the cold weather wintering grounds. Manatees rarely herd in summer like we just saw.''

''True, but there *are* exceptions,'' she insisted.

''That's correct. I just provided you with one of them.''

''You didn't!'' Geneva insisted.

''Didn't I? How do you account for those five exceptions? Or those ten exceptions?''

''I—'' She clammed up. To be perfectly honest with herself, she couldn't.

He pressed her for an answer. ''Can you account for those *fifteen* exceptions?''

''I never got an accurate count! *You're* the one who claims the manatees arrived in multiples of five, not me!''

''This is proving harder than I thought,'' Jason said,

more to himself than to her. He sighed. "I won't argue with you right now. We need to get dressed."

"We need to talk!" she insisted. Then, in a kinder voice, she said, "I mean, I really think *you* need some-one to talk to, Jase."

"Like a psychologist, perhaps? Believe me, Dr. Kelsey, I'm as sane as you. I'm also not in the market for any off-the-cuff analysis."

"But...isn't there anyone I can call for you? A wife? A girlfriend, maybe?"

He gave her that tiny, mocking smile. "My job doesn't exactly provide for girlfriends or wives."

Geneva felt an irrational flash of pleasure at this revelation, then told herself to be rational. "You could talk to me, if you want," she offered, surprising both him and her.

Jase stared at her for a moment, then shook his head. "Go get your clothes, Geneva." He urged her toward the pier with a gentle push in the small of her back, then pivoted on his heel in one graceful move-ment.

"Wait! Where are you going?" she asked, her con-cern for him warring with her concern for the mana-tees as she saw him head back toward the river. She hurried after him, all thought of changing into dry clothes forgotten.

Jase didn't stop his progress. "To look for your keys, of course."

"You do love to spin those whoppers," she said tartly. "Is this your way of changing the subject? There's no way on God's green earth you'll find my keys."

He smiled and said nothing. Geneva was beginning to recognize that slight, mocking smile of amusement.

It was definitely beginning to annoy her. She purposely stepped between him and the water's edge. "If you think you're going back to those manatees without me, you're sadly mistaken!"

Jase took another step forward. Geneva placed her hands on his chest to stop him. Immediately she knew she'd made a mistake. The look in his eyes, his quickened breathing, the sudden feel of his wet body against hers as he pulled her hard against his chest—there was no mistaking the signs.

Desire. Raw, unadulterated desire.

She tried to back away, but it was too late. His hands cupped her face and pulled her mouth closer until it was mere inches from his. Geneva saw his pupils dilate with desire and overwhelm the blue of his irises. Instead of being frightened, she was struck by the powerful beauty of those eyes. No man had ever looked at her with such naked want.

"I'm getting tired of arguing with you," he said hoarsely. "Now—just once—shut up and do what I say."

Geneva's eyes blatantly refused, although she didn't pull her face away from his touch. "This is *my* territory, Mr. Guardian. And these are *my* manatees. I don't take orders from you."

"Then you'd better learn," he said, his mouth coming down hard on hers. Geneva's breath caught in her throat as one strong hand left her face to thread itself in her hair, the other grasping her waist. Then she was clinging to him, kissing him back, her mouth allowing full possession of hers even as she possessed his.

And just when every nerve ending in Geneva's body was firing, craving more than just his kiss, when she found herself wishing for even greater closeness, greater intimacy, Jase released his willing prisoner's mouth.

"I haven't been with a woman in more than five years." His ragged words filled her ears as he nestled her closely within his thighs.

A modicum of logic returned when Geneva felt the unmistakable evidence of his response. She remained very, very still against him, but she refused to deny the pure feminine triumph that coursed through her veins. Her power over Jase Guardian was just as strong as his over her, and they both knew it.

"Five years is a long time, Geneva. I've asked you twice to get dressed," he said hoarsely. "When I get back with your keys, you'd better *be* dressed. Because if you *aren't*…"

Geneva held her breath and refused to release him.

"I sure as hell won't ask you again." At that he left her eager embrace, her balance compromised by the quickness of his departure. Geneva staggered and watched him walk back into the water with a sense of the surreal. It wasn't until he'd dived beneath it again that she hurried back to her clothes on the pier.

A scant few minutes later Geneva was dressed and waiting for him to surface. She peered anxiously into the water.

Her swollen lips and frustrated body were testimony to the man's allure, and Geneva was no schoolgirl to be unsettled by a mere kiss. *Until now*… With a sudden pang, she wondered if Jase had seen *her,* Geneva Kelsey, when he'd kissed her. Or had she just been the proverbial port in the storm after years of celibacy?

Geneva shook her head. She should be concentrating on escape, not on her kidnapper's kiss. What she ought to do was make a mad dash for the road and try to flag a ride to safety. Instead, she found herself waiting for him. For some inexplicable reason, she couldn't leave him just yet.

But where was he?

The seconds ticked by. Worried, Geneva kicked off her shoes again and was seconds away from going after him when he surfaced. She breathed a huge sigh of relief that caught in her throat as he lifted his arm out of the water, then jingled her car keys at her. Geneva's jaw dropped in amazement.

"How in the world did you find them?" she asked as he waded on shore, then joined her on the pier.

"I didn't. They were found for me." He picked up his jeans. "Turtles make great little retrievers. Their beaks are quite strong, you know."

"If—if you say so…" Geneva was too grateful to argue with him. "Thanks." She held out her hand expectantly, but Jase picked up his jeans and dropped the keys in a pocket.

"Jase!"

He stepped into his jeans. "I'll hold on to your keys for now," he remarked.

Not again! Geneva wearily rubbed her temple. "Please, Jase," she begged. "Won't you let me go home? If you really need me to believe you talk to manatees, I'll believe. If you say your mailing address is the Bermuda Triangle, I'll believe. If you say your turtles will retrieve, I'll even throw them a damn ball."

"That's not what I want."

Her voice rose in agitation. "Just what *do* you want from me?"

"I told you, Geneva. I want the Steller's sea cows."

Geneva's agitation disappeared, to be replaced by

steely determination. "You'll never get them, Jase. Do you hear me? *Never.*"

"But I will. You see, I have something you want. Something even more valuable than your precious sea cows."

"Like what? Sunken treasure ships hidden deep in your Bermuda Triangle? Riches beyond my wildest dreams? The only thing you have, Mr. Guardian, is a vivid imagination."

"You're wrong, Geneva." There it was again, that tiny, mocking smile.

"I have your brother."

Chapter Three

Jase watched the rapid play of emotions cross Geneva's lovely face. The enticing light of passion in her eyes, the pleasure from his kiss and embrace, disappeared.

The soft welcome of the lips he'd tasted was replaced by a harsh, thin line. And the hands that had tenderly wound themselves around his neck clenched into angry fists. Worst of all, the deep attraction he knew she'd felt toward him—that same attraction he'd felt himself when she'd willingly molded her pliant body to his—was gone.

First Jason saw her shocked disbelief at his mention of her brother. Then came a desperate yearning, a wild longing to believe that tore at her—and him—with unexpected sharpness. But her yearning was quickly replaced with hot fury.

"Damn you."

He winced, not at the insult but at the pain in her voice.

"Damn you to hell!"

He watched her lift her hand, and braced himself. But the slap to the face he expected—the blow she had every right to deliver and he had no right to avoid—never came.

She slowly lowered her hand and took in deep, gulping breaths. Jase watched as Geneva Kelsey fought for control. Her brown eyes were huge in the whiteness of her face. Her mouth was open, and her chest rose and fell in jerky motions. Jase wanted to take her in his arms and hold her, soothe her, comfort her.

He did none of those things. Instead, he waited.

Finally she was able to speak. "My brother is dead. He and my parents died in a plane crash on a flight to—to—" She couldn't say the word.

He finished the sentence for her. "Bermuda. A flight to Bermuda."

Geneva closed her eyes.

"I know all about you and your family, Geneva," Jase said quietly. "Your father was originally from Miami. He was a good pilot, but work was scarce. So he moved north when the Alaskan pipeline was built. He found a job, married a local woman and had two healthy children. Twins."

Geneva stood on the pier, her eyes closed, her wet bikini slowly soaking through her slacks and blouse. She was motionless, though shivering. Jase knew it would take more than a towel wrapped around her to stop it, for the trembling had nothing to do with the cold. But he said what had to be said.

"Even in his new life, Richard Kelsey never forgot his home. Every winter he flew his family to Miami for the holidays with his relatives. He loved to spend his free time flying loved ones to his favorite places. The Keys. Puerto Rico. Bermuda. And all the beautiful tropical spots found in the triangle formed by those three points.''

Geneva opened her eyes, her anger now colored with savage hate. Jase didn't hide from it. He accepted her loathing...and forced himself to continue.

''It was twenty years ago next month that fifteen-year-old Geneva Kelsey caught the flu. Twenty years ago when your father left you with your aunt and took your mother and brother for a pleasure flight. Twenty years ago when Richard Kelsey's seaplane violated the dangerous boundaries of The Sanctuary.'' Jase paused. ''And crashed.''

That finally got a reaction.

''Give me my car keys.'' She looked ghastly, but the shaking was now under control.

''I can't. I wish I could,'' he said, meaning every word of it. But he had to finish.

''Your parents died immediately upon impact. You were left with your aunt and went to school in Miami. You spent summers in Alaska with your mother's family, learning about sea life in the cold arctic waters. You became at home in two worlds.'' *Like me,* he started to say, until he realized she wouldn't appreciate the comparison.

''So at home, in fact, that you spotted the sea cows everyone else had missed. Your expertise on marine life has its roots in your childhood, as does your brother's.''

Geneva gasped as she tried to hide her interest, and failed. Jase knew that for a second she had wanted to believe him. But that willingness was gone in an instant. Still, he continued.

''Yes, Geneva. The two of you are more alike than you know. Thomas Kelsey grew up in The Sanctuary.

For two decades his knowledge of marine life has helped him fit into our society. He's still there, still alive. You can have your twin back, Geneva. Whenever you want. Just say the word.''

"In exchange for the sea cows?" she said bitterly.

"Yes."

Her lips twisted in scorn, their delicate color looking out of place on her pale face. "I haven't decided if you're truly insane, or if you're just one of those twisted people who preys on other people's misfortunes."

For a second time Jase winced, but this time not only from the pain in her voice. Even though her accusations were false, they still had the power to wound.

"Most people only extort money, not animals," she flung out. "But then, you could probably get top price for the sea cows, couldn't you?"

Jase made an involuntary movement toward her. "Geneva, please…"

Her violent "Stay away from me!' stopped him dead in his tracks.

"I'm tempted to believe you're a combination of the two," she spat out. "But for argument's sake, let's say I believe this nonsense. My twin *is* alive and well in the Bermuda Triangle."

"The Sanctuary," he corrected her.

"*Whatever.* Thomas loved me. We were close in a way that no one except other twins could understand." Her voice broke on the last words, but her eyes remained dry. "You're the man with all the answers. Tell me this. Why would he stay away for twenty years?"

"Geneva, he had no choice. The Sanctuary has its

own rules. The most important, inflexible rule of all is that our marine life, especially the species extinct in the regular world, must be protected. Any trespassers who accidentally stumble into The Sanctuary are never allowed to leave. We treat them with the same care and compassion as our marine creatures and give them the best life we possibly can, but we can never permit them to leave."

"You'd think you'd learn to lock your gates better, Mr. Guardian." The sarcasm was heavily evident, as Jase knew it was intended to be.

"We manage to keep the premises secure most of the time," he replied, "but The Sanctuary boundaries are the weakest during the winter. Most of the ships or planes missing in our vicinity are December victims that get through our boundaries. I myself found The Sanctuary then."

"But The Sanctuary let *you* out?" The sarcasm remained. "*You're* the exception?"

"Technically, no. I became a Guardian—a marine life caretaker. As such, I'm known to be trustworthy. I, and others like me, can occasionally come and go from The Sanctuary. But your brother has refused to become one of us. He thinks only of escape, with no conditions on his freedom."

Jase paused with uncharacteristic hesitation, but went on. "I'm not certain, but we think The Survivor—your brother—has held out on pledging his loyalty because of you. We think he's been waiting for you all these years, hoping you'll come for him. Thomas and you are twins, and twins are special. I'm certain Thomas knows you're alive, just as you know he's alive."

Geneva remained defiantly silent, neither confirming nor denying Jase's statement.

"He'll never find his way out, Geneva," Jase said after a moment. "Not without your help—and mine. You know my price."

Geneva shook her head. She was still shaking it when Jase reached for her.

"Don't say no just yet." He hugged her, pressing her chin against his chest to stop that determined shaking. "Think about it. Think *carefully* about it. If it's more proof you want, I'll give it to you."

But not now. He'd frightened her enough already for one day.

Geneva struggled against him. Jase instantly released her, knowing his efforts to reassure her had done just the opposite.

"You need help," she whispered, her voice hoarse. "Professional help. I hope you have the courage to find it."

Jason opened his mouth to speak, then saw she was long past hearing any more explanations. He reached into his jeans for her car keys, then took her hand and carefully placed them inside her palm.

"I need *your* help," he emphasized. "The sea cows will be *mine,* Geneva. Mine and The Sanctuary's."

"No."

"Yes. I'll give you one week to make your decision, then I'll be back for your answer." He closed her fingers around the keys.

He gestured for her to follow him off the pier. With short, jerky steps, she did, at least until she was past him. Then she stepped up her pace and hurried to her car, her wish to escape him painfully obvious.

Jase was certain that any other woman would have

run past him, dashed into the car and roared away. Geneva Kelsey did not. With the control so reminiscent of her brother, Geneva opened her door as if she hadn't a care in the world. Only the pale skin on her face and the whiteness of her knuckles around her keys gave her away. He watched with admiration for her courage, and anger at himself for not having handled this any better.

But he remained on the pier and steeled his heart for his final words.

"Remember, Geneva, *one week*. If you announce the location of the sea cows, or place them at some marine park, I'll find them."

"You'll *never* find them!"

"Oh, but I will. You see, I'm an expert yachtsman. And just before I found The Sanctuary, I sailed around the world."

Sailed away from the world, Jase silently corrected himself. *Looking for a safe harbor...and incredibly enough, finding it in The Sanctuary.*

"I'm quite familiar with Alaskan waters, Geneva. As soon as you go after those sea cows, I'll be there. And I'll be forced to steal them away."

"They might be injured! Even killed! Jase, please! No one's forcing you to do this!" Geneva insisted, her hand frozen on the open car door.

"You're wrong. I have no choice. But you do. You either help me, or you don't. If you don't help me, Geneva, this I swear. You'll never see your brother again."

"He's *dead*."

But Jase had been a trained psychologist. In another lifetime, he'd been a damned good psychologist. He heard the lie in her words, the falsehood meant to convince. For the first time since he'd met her, he felt hope.

"He's *alive*."

This time Geneva Kelsey didn't argue with him. She climbed into the car, started the engine and drove away.

Jase watched until the car and its driver were long out of sight. "Oh, yes, Geneva. He's very much alive," he said softly.

He was positive that, in the curious way of twins, she knew it, too....

GENEVA RUBBED at her computer-strained eyes and wished like hell whoever it was she'd met four days ago had given her his real name.

Four days... Had it only been four days since her world had been turned upside down by a mysterious stranger, a stranger who had both shocked and intrigued her? The memory of his kiss was still with her. In any other circumstances, Geneva would have eagerly welcomed, even pursued, a future that her time with Jase had hinted at.

But these circumstances were hardly ordinary. The man she was interested in claimed he talked to animals, was from the Bermuda Triangle and knew her long-lost twin brother. To top it all off, she didn't even know his real name.

After one day spent in the Sirenian Institute's library, another spent at the state archives, and yet a third wasted phoning all her university contacts, she'd come to the inescapable conclusion that Jase Guardian didn't exist. Not on paper, not in the computer, not in anyone's memories. Marine biologists were common in Florida, but sirenian experts were an elite group.

Geneva knew most of them by name, or at least could find someone who knew the ones she didn't.

That wasn't the case this time. So here she was now, back at the library, trying not to feel idiotic researching the Bermuda Triangle. Normally, wild horses couldn't have dragged her to the reference section where the books on that particular subject were kept, but her desperate wish to see her twin again forced her hand. And if she was honest with herself, she'd admit that her fascination for this mysterious man also played a part in her being here.

Feeling slightly foolish, Geneva opened her books and began to read. All the books agreed that the Bermuda Triangle apexes were listed as Miami, Florida; San Juan, Puerto Rico; and Bermuda. After those easily accepted facts, the rest of the material she read was pure speculation.

Most of the books were so utterly unscientific that ordinarily she would never have read past the first page, let alone the first chapter. Stories about secret nuclear test sites, lost underwater cities like Atlantis, haunted ships from the Sargasso Sea, and UFOs preying upon "Devil's Triangle" victims were not Geneva's idea of a fun afternoon.

And none of these theories jibed with Jase's benevolent version of Sanctuary paradise. In fact, after reading some of the more outlandish tales, Geneva found Jase's version the easiest to accept. She certainly wasn't ready to trust him yet, but after feeling his very human, very masculine body against hers, she was prepared to swear on a bible that Jase was no UFO alien.

However, there were certain inescapable facts. The military had lost both ships and aircraft in the Triangle without a trace, as had commercial airlines. Geneva was surprised to find that the records of U.S. losses started in 1800, when the USS *Pickering* disappeared with a crew of ninety men.

Geneva's eyes scanned the victims' list, which cautioned that these were the *known* victims from an era when record-keeping was haphazard at best. Despite her skepticism about any supernatural properties of the area, she couldn't help being affected by the stark statistics.

1814: The USS *Wasp* disappeared with 140 sailors.
1824: The USS *Wild Cat* vanished with its fourteen-man crew.
1843: The USS *Grampus* was lost.
1910: The Navy tug USS *Nina* disappeared.

And the list went on and on with British naval ships, Japanese freighters and ships from other countries missing as well, along with their entire crews.

All of the books Geneva read listed the loss of the USS *Cyclops* as one of the Navy's most baffling mysteries. No trace of the Navy coal ship or crew was found, even though a massive search was made for the 308-man crew, which included VIP passenger Consul General Alfred Gottschalk.

By 1921 so many vessels from so many nations had vanished in the Triangle that the U.S. government had five different departments investigating.

Geneva scanned the most recent list, eagerly searching for Jase's name. She'd hoped to make a list of the missing vessels—especially missing yachts—from five years ago, which was when Jase claimed to have found The Sanctuary. Maybe she could discover his last name, too. Unfortunately, the most current book was eight years old and was of no help at all. The library's card catalog listed no other new copies.

Geneva pushed aside her disappointment and continued with her research. When the golden age of aviation arrived, so did more victims of the Triangle. Navy and air force planes disappeared. Commercial flights such as the 1948 British-South American Airways *Star Tiger* or a 1972 Flamingo Airlines plane met the same fate. And, of course, private planes such as Geneva's father's had to be counted among the victims.

Her parents' deaths might have been the most painful, but Geneva saw that the December 4, 1945, disappearance of six Navy planes from Fort Lauderdale's Naval Air Station was the most famous. The planes had filed a triangular flight path on their routine training mission before they vanished. The Martin Mariner rescue plan with a thirteen-man crew dispatched to find them also vanished.

Newspapers immediately labeled the doomed triangular flight path as "The Triangle of Death." Later, when Bermuda was noticed to be the northern boundary of the victim-claiming area, a legend was born.

A legend...or a carefully hidden marine sanctuary with carefully trained guardians like Jase?

Geneva shook her head and closed the book. Her scientific mind wasn't ready to accept the library books' explanations, or Jase's, either. Discouraged that she hadn't found anything of use, especially Jase's full name, she walked the book and its companions back to the nonfiction section.

She'd have to stop at a bookstore and order a newer Bermuda Triangle publication, one that would list the missing vessels from five years ago. Perhaps she could discover who he was that way. Her present sources were useless. Not only had the text not revealed Jase's true identity, they hadn't described the Bermuda Triangle phenomenon to her satisfaction.

Even the more reputable library sources had very few hypotheses that marine-expert Geneva hadn't already made herself. The violent Caribbean-Atlantic weather patterns with their hurricanes, electrical and thunderstorms and water spouts didn't need the supernatural's help to sink ships or crash planes. And navigation could be tricky among the Triangle's many islands. Shallow shoals in the Caribbean could rip out a hull, as the Spanish treasure galleons had found to their sorrow. From there, even a modern vessel could sink to some of the deepest marine trenches in the world, if the swift, turbulent Gulf Stream didn't quickly erase any traces of wreckage first.

"No books to check out? Or did you find what you were looking for?" the reference librarian asked as Geneva headed toward the exit.

Geneva didn't know how to answer that. "I found a few things of interest," she lied. She'd found nothing, read nothing, learned nothing, that could help her.

Except, perhaps, one tiny fact. The books said most of the missing vessels and planes were lost during the violent winter storms. December was an especially fatal month for victims. Yet it was each year in December that she was most certain Thomas was alive.

They were twins. They'd always had a close bond— not a telepathic thing like popular science fiction books described. But there was a definite empathy between them, an empathy that let one know when the other twin was unhappy, or hurt, or sick or—Geneva was positive—dead. Yet in December Geneva was always certain that her brother was alive. She could almost *feel* his presence.

Her relatives from both sides of the family said it was wishful thinking. After all, December was when her parents' plane went missing. But if just for a moment she put the whole thing in Jase Guardian's context of the Triangle...

"We manage to keep the premises secure most of the time, but The Sanctuary boundaries are the weakest during the winter. Most of the ships or planes that are lost in our vicinity are December victims who get through the boundaries. I myself found The Sanctuary then."

Could it be possible that Geneva Kelsey could only empathically sense Thomas Kelsey when The Sanctuary barriers were *down* in December? Could their "twin thing," as Thomas used to call it, only work then?

Could it actually be possible that her brother was still alive?

"This is crazy!" she said out loud in the parking lot. "*I'm* crazy!" She tried to push the thought from her mind.

But she couldn't. She kept remembering the sincerity in Jase's eyes when he'd spoken to her on the pier, or the heady feel of his lips moving over hers. Her physical and emotional reaction to him was confusing enough. She couldn't explain that any more than she could explain how all those manatees appeared where they shouldn't have been. Or how Jase had found those car keys she'd hurled with all her strength into a weed-choked, muddy-bottomed river. There had to be *some* logical explanation for the strange events of that day—and for the man himself.

Not knowing that explanation was driving her crazy!

Long before the week he'd given her was up, Geneva had made up her mind. When he showed up again, she wasn't calling the police. She wouldn't even recommend a good psychiatrist.

Not until she heard exactly what else Jase Guardian had to say...

FOR THE FIRST TIME in five years, the lush tropical beauty of his island didn't soothe Jase's spirits. He tossed and turned in his hammock. No matter that this was the time he usually took his afternoon nap in preparation for his work among the nocturnal ocean creatures. No matter that the ocean breeze was cool and relaxing. He couldn't sleep. He hadn't been able to sleep well in the two days since he'd left Geneva Kelsey at the pier.

Oh, he'd tried. But for the longest time her exotic face kept him awake. He'd revel in the beauty of it...then he'd remember how his words had wiped off that lovely, serene expression and replaced it with shock, fury and hate. And then, when he finally *had* fallen asleep, he hadn't been able to *stay* asleep.

He'd had sensuous, erotic dreams of that lissome, curving body pressed firmly against his in the waters of the St. Johns. He could again feel the delicate ridges of her ribs as his hands spanned her waist, feel the softness of her breasts against his chest. His sleeping body twitched with memory at the way her hips had nestled so comfortably against his thighs, the way her ebony hair had draped over her shoulders.

He'd woken from a restless sleep to the hard, throbbing evidence that his long-absent libido had definitely returned—evidence that didn't disappear when he'd forgone his usual afternoon nap to swim laps in the lagoon. It had been so long since he'd held a woman— any woman—in his arms. And now that he finally had, it had felt so very good...and been all too brief.

Jase swam even faster in the water, reminding himself that he and Geneva were from two different worlds. His contact with her was strictly business. The Sanctuary always made good on its bargains: in this case, the sea cows for Thomas Kelsey's freedom.

Nothing lasting could ever come of this attraction, Jase told himself. If he wanted a woman in his life, he had plenty of interested females to choose from right here in The Sanctuary. It would certainly make more sense to pursue one of them instead of an outsider. But for once logic meant absolutely nothing to Jase. Something that had nothing to do with logic couldn't wait to see Geneva again. To hold her again. And to feel her willing lips open for his possession.

Just as he wanted to possess the rest of her...

Jase clenched his cupped hands into fists in frustration and gave up on the idea of swimming. He headed for the small bungalow that was his home and dried his frustrated body with a towel. Until he'd met Geneva Kelsey, he hadn't bothered thinking about his sexuality. Or his lack of it. Instead, he'd spent those years contemplating the agonies of his very own personal hell. There was very little room in hell for pleasure.

Jase crossed to the desk in the open living room with its huge glass windows and view of the lagoon. On impulse, he removed the file full of newspaper clippings in the bottom drawer—the clippings that told of the last woman he'd cared for deeply.

And killed.

He settled down cross-legged on the hardwood floor's woven straw mat and spread the newspaper clippings around in chronological order. "Dr. Jason Merrick opens innovative new clinic for autistic children..." "Doctor of autistic brother Shawn Merrick has personal stake in popular clinic. Noted psychologist claims dolphin/autistic children pairing is breakthrough therapy...." "Success of Merrick's autism cures shadowed by animal rights activists! Group claims cruelty to dolphins...." "Jason Merrick of controversial clinic steps up security and gets restraining order against HADES (Humans Against Dolphin Exploitation Society). HADES threatens retaliation...."

And then, the boldest, most violent words of all.

"Clinic therapist and dolphins slaughtered by bomb explosion! HADES activists arrested for terrorism...."

Jase forced himself to read on, remembering Nanci Wheeling, the therapist he'd hired, then dated. Theirs was no great love affair, but they enjoyed much more than a boss and employee relationship. At Nanci's urging, Jase had enjoyed Nanci's company off the clock and—again at her request—occasionally her bed. Both valued their friendship. So much so, in fact, that Nanci hadn't minded staying late at work that fateful night when Jase had needed extra help working with the dolphins.

She'd paid the ultimate price for her generosity. And the newspapers had a field day, Jase remembered.

"Dr. Jason Merrick sued by Nanci Wheeling's grief-stricken parents for criminal negligence...." "HADES found guilty in therapist and dolphin deaths.

Psychologist's security measures found adequate. Dr. Jason Merrick found not guilty of negligence...."

And in smaller, less dramatic headlines... "Merrick announces clinic will not reopen."

A few months later, the final death knell. "Police report the disappearance of Dr. Jason Merrick, the controversial owner of the nationally known autism clinic. Dr. Merrick, credited with repeated cures of autistic children by using dolphin's special communication abilities, has vanished from his Miami home. Police suspect foul play."

Jason rested his chin on one knee, his long brown hair falling forward at the motion as he remembered it all....

It wasn't foul play that caused his disappearance. It was craziness. His own craziness and guilt. Because in a cruel, ironic twist of fate, Nanci had died, all his dolphins had died, and Dr. Jason Merrick had walked away untouched.

And then he'd climbed into his yacht and sailed away, far away from the irony of a bomb that had killed the innocent and destroyed his life's work. Jase studied the last newspaper clipping without moving from his spot on the mat. "The Coast Guard reports expert yachtsman Dr. Jason Merrick missing at sea. Vast Merrick estate falls into hands of autistic, institutionalized brother. Court-appointed guardian chosen..."

Jase had found The Sanctuary soon after. He'd been desperate for his own personal refuge, and actually finding one seemed like a dream come true. There, within the boundaries of the luxuriant marine preserve, The Sanctuary had worked its tropical magic. Jase had

been able to find a small amount of peace for his tor-
tured soul.

He'd thrown himself into his new work and given
up on the real world. His ties to Florida were fragile
at best. His parents had long ago divorced due to the
strain of raising, then institutionalizing, an autistic
child. They led their own separate lives. Even before
his work was destroyed, Jase had never been able to
help his brother Shawn. With the destruction of his
clinic, Jason knew Shawn would forever remain in his
silent, withdrawn world. All in all, there'd been nothing to lure Dr. Jason Merrick back.

So Jase had kept busy in The Sanctuary, even as
he'd kept to himself. Because of his parents' failed
marriage and his guilt over Nanci's death, he'd sworn
off women....

Until now. Until he'd met Geneva Kelsey.

Suddenly his solitude wasn't a comfort—it was a
curse. He wanted Geneva back in his arms with an
intensity that overrode the fact that they'd never have
a long-term relationship like he could have with a
Sanctuary woman. But there it was. He didn't *want* a
Sanctuary woman. He wanted Geneva.

Opening old wounds regarding her brother, however, hadn't helped matters. Fortunately or unfortunately for Jase, Geneva Kelsey really did have the best
interests of the sea cows at heart. Jase scooped up the
clippings, including the one with the photo of Nanci
and shoved them carelessly back into his desk.

"I may have to bring her here," he said aloud. His
newly awakened body surged at the thought of Geneva
here on his island. Jase smiled, the image of her—
better yet, of *them*—filling his mind.

"Soon..."

Chapter Four

"Manatees and conservation for Clay County elementary schoolchildren. East amphitheater. Presentation by Dr. G. Kelsey at 10:00 a.m."

Jase quickly checked the position of the sun—he didn't use a watch to tell time anymore—and saw that it was almost ten now. After a glance at the map on the back of the flier, he hurried toward the east end of the marine park.

The presentation was just starting when Jase arrived. All of the front row seats of the outdoor amphitheater were filled by schoolchildren. Jase climbed the stairs and took a seat in one of the higher back rows just as Geneva came out amid the sound of applause. She stepped onto a podium in the freshwater tank, separated from her audience by a Plexiglas plate.

"Thank you for that warm welcome, boys and girls. I'm Dr. Kelsey of the Florida Sirenian Institute. And if you'll look carefully through the Plexiglas sides of the tank, I'll introduce you to Marnee."

There were "oohs" and "ahs" as the children did just that. Not only could Jase sense the single female manatee in the tank, he could easily see her from his position. But for once his mind wasn't on a marine dweller. His concentration was totally on Geneva. She was just as lovely as he remembered, even in a blue neoprene shortie—a legless, short-sleeved wet suit preferred by divers in the warm Florida waters. Her hair was in one long braid that hung almost to her waist, and she held a waterproof cordless microphone in one hand. Jason suddenly found himself remembering when that graceful hand had cradled his neck as he'd kissed her.

"Marnee is one of our manatees," Geneva continued. "And manatees are mammals. Who knows what that means? That's right..." she replied to the correctly shouted answers. "Marnee is a mammal from the order Sirenia, which is why this marine park is called the Sirenian Institute."

There were a few understanding nods from the audience. Jase watched her establish an instant rapport with the children. Obviously he wasn't the only person captivated by Geneva Kelsey's genuine charm.

"You'll see that manatees have large, seallike bodies," Geneva pointed out. "But if you all look closely, you'll notice the differences. For one thing, their tails are spatulate. You know, like the round spatulas your mothers cook hamburgers with."

Jase smiled at her choice of words. He'd never heard manatees compared with kitchen utensils before.

"Seals are saltwater dwellers and have what are called split-tail flukes. The Florida manatee, which technically is called a West Indian manatee, is freshwater dwelling, and their tails are rounded."

The Steller's sea cows have split-tail flukes, Geneva, Jase wanted to say aloud. Then, annoyed at himself for letting business intrude and draw his attention away from Geneva, he tried to get his thoughts off the Steller's sea cows by once again concentrating on the manatee in the tank. He knew she'd stay at the bottom for fifteen minutes or so before surfacing, as compared to surfacing every few minutes when active. Jase was about to make direct mental contact when Geneva's voice distracted him again.

"Marnee is young and only about five feet long. On the average, though, manatees are about nine feet long and weigh about 1,000 pounds," Geneva continued. "Imagine seven of the teachers here combined into one big fat lump. That's an average manatee weight."

There were giggles from the children as each class stared at their own teacher and tried to imagine him or her lumped with six others. Jase himself laughed at Geneva's cleverness and the children's reactions. The rusty, unfamiliar sound in his throat startled him. *Dear lord, how long has it been since I've laughed?*

With that realization, he completely gave up on concentrating on the manatee. Geneva Kelsey was just too distracting—too captivating—right now. She had a stage presence about her that was charming those kids right out of their seats. And him too, if he was honest with himself.

Geneva stepped down from her podium and waded out into the water to get closer to her audience. "Here's a question for you. Are the manatees endangered? Yes or no?"

"Yes!" the children yelled out.

"Very good. Who knows why they're endangered?"

"Destruction of the Everglades!" some children yelled out. "Pollution!" and "Boats!" yelled others.

Jase watched Geneva nod. "Correct. Boat traffic is the biggest killer of manatees. Right now there are only about twelve-hundred manatees in Florida. The manatee is the most endangered marine mammal in the United States."

Suddenly it was very quiet in the outdoor amphitheater. Jase could hear Geneva's every word. Even though Geneva wasn't telling him anything he didn't know, he couldn't help but be affected by her passion for her work, her dedication to saving the marine creatures.

We're more alike than you know, Geneva. That thought gave him satisfaction. They might be from two totally different worlds, but they did share a common bond, a deep love of the sea's inhabitants. That made the gulf between Jase Guardian of The Sanctuary and Geneva Kelsey of the Florida Sirenian Institute seem a little narrower. A smile crossed his face as Jase hung on to Geneva's every word.

"You see, manatees are very slow moving. They can't get out of the way of Florida boat traffic. The boat propellers can hurt them, or kill them. That's why Marnee is here. Look at her back. See all those gouges?"

The children did.

"Those were made by a boat that ran over her. She's better now," Geneva said quietly. "We were able to help her, but those scars will never go away. We don't want that to happen to other manatees, do we?"

The audience gave her a collective "No!"

"Good. Then let me tell you what you can do to help."

Jase listened as Geneva went over simple conservation efforts the children could perform. He saw the attentive expressions on the children's faces and admired Geneva for her honesty. He knew educating children on the cruelties of life wasn't easy.

"Ask your parents to get a Save the Manatee license plate instead of a regular Florida plate. The extra money goes to places like this institute. I have one on my car. Who's got one on theirs?"

A scant ten hands of students from a dozen classrooms went up.

"You children have your *own cars?*" Geneva asked with feigned amazement.

The audience suddenly burst into laughter. Half the ten tried to explain that it was a parent's car, while the other half pretended to really own a car. Either way, Jase saw that the worried looks of the children were now gone. He looked at Geneva with new respect. She was amazing. Children in today's modern world had enough trauma in their lives, but Geneva had gotten her point across without any needless emotional battering.

Geneva waited until the laughter died down. "Okay, so I misunderstood. However, those of you whose *families* have manatee license plates get gold stars." She allowed the lucky children to preen a few seconds, then continued. "You see, manatees only have babies every two to five years. So we have to be very careful that more don't die than are born. If we can do that, our manatees will be all right. We don't want them to end up like—"

Jase saw Geneva hesitate. He knew exactly why she hesitated.

"Like other extinct species, such as the passenger pigeon or the dodo bird."

Like the Steller's sea cows, Jase silently corrected her.

"Now, if you'll follow your teachers to our auditorium, we have a movie to show you. You'll be able to see the manatees close up. Thank you for coming today, boys and girls. I hope you come back again really soon."

Applause was followed by the chatter of excited children as they allowed the teachers to herd them into single file and then began the trek toward the auditorium. Jase watched Geneva a moment longer before starting down the stairs. He'd only made it halfway down before he saw Geneva's chin jerk sharply up. So, she'd finally noticed him. At least she wasn't running for the nearest phone, he thought with satisfaction.

Jase stepped all the way down and leaned against the top of the Plexiglas. "Hello, Geneva."

She nodded, then replaced the cordless microphone in its slot on the podium. "Has it been a week already?" she asked, her chilly voice carrying easily across the freshwater tank separating them.

Despite her tone, Jase saw a momentary warmth in her eyes, and he found himself smiling ever so slightly. *Unless he was sadly mistaken—and he didn't think he was—she'd counted the days just as he had.* "I enjoyed your talk to the children. You're very good with them."

Geneva shrugged off his compliments with a stiff movement of her shoulders.

"How do I get over to you?" he asked.

Geneva hesitated. "Unauthorized personnel aren't allowed back here."

"Are you going to make me swim over to you?"

"No, don't," Geneva immediately said. "Security would be here in a second. Come around back and to the left. I'll let you in."

Jase felt a thrill of satisfaction as she left her concrete island's shoreline and disappeared from sight. If she wasn't willing to call the guards on him—wasn't willing to lose a chance at finding her missing twin—perhaps she was in the mood to listen. At last he was making progress. He hurried over to the locked gate, heard the electronic whine as the lock was disengaged and stepped inside the marine tank premises.

His sensitive hearing could detect the underwater squeaks and squeals of other manatees. There must be smaller holding tanks out back.

She motioned him over to an aluminum observation walkway that traversed the main viewing tank and led to the concrete island.

"Those other manatees seem crowded. Why don't you open the back tank gates and let the others into the main tank?" Jase asked as she came closer.

Geneva visibly started. Jase saw the surprise and confusion cross her face. He could tell from the wary look in her eyes that she still didn't trust him.

"How do you know that?" Geneva asked. "I never said there were other manatees here."

Jase gave her a telling look.

"Come on, Jase, you don't really expect me to believe that you are what you claim to be."

"And what's that?"

Her eyebrows drew together with disapproval. "You know—some mysterious man who can talk to the animals."

"But I can." Unwilling to walk on the slippery, wet walkway in shoes, Jase kicked off his Dock-sides and picked them up, all the while concentrating. "There's...one male calf and two females here, three if you count Marnee in the front holding tank."

Geneva's jaw dropped. "Who told you that?"

"No one."

"Don't lie to me. I know you've never been back there. *Someone* had to have told you."

"Someone did. The manatees themselves." Jase hid a smile of amusement at Geneva's confusion, crossed over to her side of the walkway and followed her onto the concrete island. The island was connected to a separating partition and tunnel that hid the smaller back tanks from the larger front tank.

Geneva hurried after him. "And just *how* did they do that?"

"It's kind of hard to explain." Jase dropped his shoes onto a dry patch, then leaned against the podium.

"I'm listening."

"Well, the higher the life form, the better the communication. For very basic sea life, such as sponges or jellyfish, I can only sense very basic elements. Hunger's easy to pick up. So is injury and death, and of course the reproductive phases are always strong. Not much else is."

Jase began to unbutton his shirt. The new clothes provided for his trip away from The Sanctuary felt stiff and scratchy. "For creatures with higher intelligence, such as those in the order Cetacea—you know, the whales, the dolphins and porpoises—"

"I know what cetaceans are!" was Geneva's tart response.

"Of course you do. Sorry." Jase flashed her an apologetic grin, then continued unbuttoning his shirt.

"The higher cetaceans are much more complex. So is the communication. I can't pick up their exact language, of course. Neither can they pick up mine. But somehow my mental images and their verbal sounds and nonverbal sonar find a common denominator. I'm able to empathize with them to a much greater extent than the lower species. My empathy is returned in direct proportion."

Jase watched Geneva's eyes open wide with comprehension. "Like me and Thomas. He—we could converse without talking. Thomas used to call it our 'twin thing.'"

She broke off abruptly, then averted her gaze and toyed with the zipper on her wet suit. Jase feared he'd reopened old wounds again until the pensive expression on Geneva's face changed.

"I read somewhere—oh, years ago—about someone doing work with cetaceans. Whoever it was kept using those words."

"What words?"

"Common denominator. For some reason, the phrase sticks in my head."

Common denominator. Jase felt an icy shaft of fear deep in his chest. That was *his* favorite catchphrase when describing his work. Or rather, Dr. Jason Merrick's work. Geneva couldn't have been referring to anyone else's words but his.

"I wish I could remember who it was...." Geneva's voice drifted off.

Who would have guessed a sirenian biologist would have read—and remembered—his articles on dolphins and autism? That had been over five years ago. Jase desperately prayed her memory had become hazy with the passage of time.

"You wouldn't happen to have read that article, would you?" Geneva asked.

Jase forced himself to meet her gaze, praying he wouldn't see condemnation in her eyes. He saw only her frustration at not being able to remember. Nothing more. Jase slowly exhaled, carefully hiding his relief. He even managed to pull off his shirt nonchalantly and toss it over with his shoes.

"Well?" she urged.

"No, I haven't read it." That much was the truth. He hadn't read it. He'd written it. "And I'm not here to discuss outdated scientific tomes. I'm here to convince you I am what I say I am. You make up the tests this time, and you decide if I pass muster." He deliberately unbuckled his belt and unzipped his jeans.

Geneva was sufficiently distracted by his actions to drop the previous subject. "Wait!" she hissed.

Jase momentarily paused. "What?"

"Let me get you a shortie." Her voice dropped even lower as she nervously looked around. "You can't go swimming around half-naked in my tanks! I've got another group of schoolchildren in a half hour, and I've seen your version of underwear!"

"Relax." Jase let his jeans fall to his ankles and stepped out of them, exposing men's swimming briefs, a recent clothing purchase he'd dug out earlier from his newly stocked suitcase. "I'm decent."

"Decent?" Geneva's eyes dropped to his crotch. "Not for schoolchildren, you aren't! If that spandex were any tighter, they'd all be getting a lesson in human anatomy instead of sirenian anatomy."

"And if you keep staring at me like that, you'll be getting a lesson in male sexual response," he retorted. He watched her eyes immediately snap back up to his face. "You can either get in the water with me, Geneva, or my *spandex* can remind you about those long years I've spent without—"

Geneva's body hit the water with a splash.

"—a woman." Jase grinned. He allowed himself the luxury of watching her body knife down through the water then up to the surface before joining her himself. He was still grinning as he swam over to her, not even bothering to keep his amusement in check. He'd rather see Geneva's hot temper than the fear he'd caused at his last visit.

"Let's go see Marnee," Jase suggested as he kicked over to her side with easy strokes. "I'll see if I can strike up a conversation with her."

"You'll *see*?" Geneva floated easily, the buoyancy of her wet suit eliminating the need for her to tread water as he was. "Does this mean the creatures of the deep might *just possibly* refuse to converse with Mr. Mystical from The Sanctuary?"

Instead of being offended by her sarcasm, Jase was pleased by her use of the marine preserve's correct name. His good mood that had dimmed at her vague recollection of his old article was back in full force. So full, in fact, that his cheerful face immediately registered a suspicious look from Geneva.

"What now?" he asked tolerantly.

"I don't like it when you look so smug."

"Dr. Kelsey, you're a hard woman to please." Jase gestured toward her buoyant wet suit. "And you're also not going to be able to dive in that shortie. Take it off and join me."

After making certain Geneva was following his instructions, Jase dove toward the still-resting manatee. The water in the tank was thirty feet deep, but Marnee was resting on a ledge down about fifteen feet. Jase concentrated on sending out reassuring messages of safety as he approached her.

Jase received no sensation of panic from the manatee, so he remained below the surface. As he kicked his legs to keep from floating upward again, he wished some of his dolphins were around to keep him underwater. Barring that impossibility, he wondered if Geneva had a weight belt he could borrow.

His body was still occupied with the task of keeping an even depth when he felt the manatee's mind reach out for his. Jase remained in place, even when Geneva reached his side. He was vibrantly aware of the water's displacement, signaling every movement of her lithe, maillot-clothed body. Her presence almost detracted from his awareness of the manatee's growing interest—and distress.

Jase forced his attention away from Geneva and concentrated harder. Suddenly he felt a burst of transmitted pain—a sharp abdominal knifing that took him unawares. He flinched at first, then opened his mind to accept the message with even greater clarity. He felt a strong maternal longing, a longing that was pathetically unfulfilled, and suddenly he knew what was wrong....

Geneva followed Jase up as he surfaced and was beside him all the way over to the concrete shoreline. She grabbed his arm when he stumbled getting out.

"Jase? Jase, are you okay?" she asked frantically, helping him down to the concrete ground when he staggered.

Jase nodded, but Geneva wasn't about to settle for his answer.

"Are you *sure?*"

"Yes."

"Like hell you are. You don't look okay to me. In fact, you look like you're going to pass out." She sank to his side and pressed his head down toward his knees. "Deep breaths," she urged as she massaged his shoulders. Geneva felt her chest tighten with fear. If anything happened to this man, the man who just might hold her twin's fate in his hands...

"And you yelled at *me* for staying under water too long at the pier," she said, her voice trembling, her eyes dark with concern. "Breathe, Jase! I can see the headlines now. Prominent sirenian expert loses job letting unauthorized Dr. Doolittle drown with manatee."

Geneva watched Jase lift his head at that and swiveled around to face her. "Dr. Doolittle?"

"Yeah. You know. The musical about the guy who talked to the animals. I think the movie starred Rex Harrison." Geneva nervously pushed her dripping bangs back, then resumed rubbing his broad shoulders. "I saw it when I was a kid."

"It's been a long time since anyone called me Doctor," Jase said slowly. "Dr. Doolittle...I think I like that."

"Yeah, well, I don't like you trying to kill yourself in my pool." She slapped his arm, but her blow held no more sting than her shaky voice.

Jase reached for her hands and pulled her around directly in front of him. "I wasn't anywhere near death, Geneva. But Marnee is. She's got a massive infection."

Geneva blinked with surprise. "I know she's running a fever, Jase, but that's just a residual effect from the propeller gouges. She's on antibiotics. The wounds themselves are healing nicely. Marnee's just taking a little longer to bounce back.''

Jason shook his head. "No. Sometime between the boat injury and her relocation here, this female gave birth. I'd guess the labor was brought on early by the collision. Geneva, she didn't expel all of the placenta. She's suffering complications from a putrid, virulent uterus.''

Geneva's mouth dropped open, then closed again.

"I wasn't out of breath. That's not why I was so shook up. It wasn't the lack of air, it was the pain! The *manatee's* pain. She let me feel how she feels.'' Geneva saw Jase shiver. "Geneva, you have to help her!''

"Jase, she's fine,'' Geneva insisted.

Jase shook his head. "She's not. Either you help her, or I'm going back down there and putting her down.'' He shook Geneva for emphasis. Once. *Hard.* "Don't you see? She's in agony!''

Geneva stood up and backed away from him. Her brown eyes were huge as she stared, her hand over her mouth.

"I'm not crazy, Geneva. I swear to God I'm not.''

There was a long pause.

"It's easy enough to find out if I'm right. Go get one of your staff vets.''

Geneva dropped her hand from her mouth. "And just what am I supposed to tell them? That a man from the Bermuda Triangle thinks Marnee needs more medical attention? That Marnee told you this herself?''

"I don't care what excuse you use! Just tell them to come and check her!''

"They'll think I'm mad!''

"I've never lied to you. Please, Geneva, you have to trust me!" he said frantically.

She stared at him, her mind in a whirl. Could she trust this man—a man who claimed to be able to talk to animals, a man who said he knew her long-lost brother was alive? Dare she put her professional reputation at stake? Geneva bit her lower lip, then spoke.

"*If* I go, will you promise not to hurt Marnee while I'm gone?"

"You believe me?"

"I—I don't know," she replied more calmly than she felt. "But I'll get the vets, anyway. I want your word of honor you won't touch Marnee while I'm gone. In fact, I want you to promise you won't even get back in the water. Swear it, Jase, or I call security this minute."

"I promise."

Geneva nodded. She didn't understand why she was able to accept his word on face value, but there was something about him, something in his eyes, that convinced her he meant what he said.

"Okay, then. If security hassles you, just tell them to call the vet's office and ask for me. They know the number." She started off, then stopped. "Will you be all right if I leave you here alone? You're not going to pass out or anything?" The thought of Jase sick was just as unsettling as the possibility of Marnee being ill. Perhaps more so...

"No."

"Are you *sure?* Maybe you should come with me to the clinic and let one of the vets check you out. Frankly, you look like hell."

"Don't you understand? I *look* like Marnee *feels!* Just go!"

And this time, she left.

Geneva hurried away, but the closer she got to the vet's office, the more confused she became. Was she actually going to disturb staff on the say-so of one mysterious man? Was she crazy for listening to him? And then, because Geneva was always honest with herself, she asked herself the million-dollar question.

Was her attraction to him getting the best of her? Had his bewitching eyes and voice, the taste of his lips, the feel of his fingers in her hair, his body pressed against hers, affected her judgment?

She refused to hide from the truth. The answer was a resounding *yes*. And that answer both frightened and excited her. There was so very much at stake here. If Jase was telling the truth about Marnee, then he could be telling the truth about Thomas. About The Sanctuary. About *everything*…

All right, Geneva, this is it, she thought as she hurried her pace. *If Jase is right about Marnee—if the staff vets confirm his diagnosis—pragmatic scientist or not, I'll trust him.*

Geneva felt a momentary pang at the thought of the Steller's sea cows. She'd have to give them up. Her career would certainly suffer a setback when the cows "disappeared," to say nothing of her conservation plans to breed a healthy population. But on the plus side, she'd have Thomas…and she'd get to learn more about Jase.

And as reckless, even as dangerous as it was, she was determined to learn more about Jase.

Two staff vets followed Geneva back to the tank. As they approached, Geneva saw that Jase was sitting quietly, the manatee on the shoreline at his feet as she and the vets crossed over the aluminum walkway.

Jase gently stroked the manatee's massive head. Geneva wondered how he'd managed to get the manatee so close, for manatees usually avoided beaching themselves on shorelines. Her stomach was in knots. On one hand she certainly wanted Marnee to be healthy, but on the other hand she desperately wanted to believe in Jase. So she said nothing. She let the vets do their job, noticing that Jase stayed near Marnee during the tranquilization process and subsequent examination.

Finally the verdict was pronounced.

"You were right, Geneva," the female vet said. "Her uterus is badly infected. Another few days and this cow would have died."

Her breath caught in her throat. Geneva's gaze immediately flew to Jase's. *He was right! He hadn't lied, after all!*

"The antibiotics for the propeller gashes masked the other symptoms," said the other vet. "Good call, Dr. Kelsey."

Geneva started to protest that she *hadn't* made the call, but at Jase's warning look, was silent once more. She stared at him as more help was called for. Marnee was transferred to the hospital tanks and the competent hands of the Sirenian Institute vets. Jase and Geneva were left alone.

"Do you—do you think they caught the infection in time?" Geneva's voice was unsteady.

Jase dropped a reassuring hand onto her shoulder. "I'm sure of it. I'm certain she'll be able to successfully conceive again and carry full term."

Geneva lifted grateful eyes to his. "Thank you, Jase. From both me and Marnee."

"You're very welcome. I'm glad I could help."

Geneva felt her shoulder warm under his touch. "You shouldn't have let me take the credit, Jase. It was your diagnosis, not mine."

"Well, I could hardly expect you to give them the correct explanation, now, could I?" he asked kindly. "Don't worry about giving credit where credit is due. The most important thing is getting Marnee well. And she *will* get well, Geneva. I'm positive."

Geneva's throat felt tight. She couldn't speak the words to show her gratitude. Instead, she threw her arms around his neck and hugged him. Immediately she felt his arms encircle her waist.

"Thanks for saving her," she whispered, her head on his shoulder. "To think I had her here on display all this time and didn't know how much she was suffering...."

"It's all right, Geneva." He stroked her hair. "You couldn't have known. You're not a Guardian."

Geneva backed away from him and met his gaze again. "But you are." Her quiet words rang with conviction.

"Yes."

"And you really can understand the marine animals." A statement, not a question.

"Yes, Geneva. I can."

She thought about that, eyebrows furrowed, lips compressed in a pensive line. "Have you ever talked to Steller's sea cows before?"

"No. I've never been in contact with them. We thought they were extinct."

"But *could* you?"

"I think so."

Geneva tilted her head, her eyes still intently on his.

"This place in the Bermuda Triangle, Jase. This Sanctuary…"

"Yes?"

"I want you to take me there."

Chapter Five

"You're really going on vacation?" the young secretary asked in disbelief as Geneva checked her messages. "This is actually your last day at work for the next two weeks?"

"It is." Geneva scribbled response after response to the messages as quickly as she could. Today was the day she'd promised to meet Jase in Miami; the day he'd promised to take her to The Sanctuary...and Thomas. The *last* thing she needed was countless phone messages and a chatty secretary to slow her down.

"Well, I'm curious. You just got back from vacation in Alaska. You never go to Bermuda this time of year."

The Sanctuary is hardly a place you'll find in the summer travel brochures, Geneva thought to herself, scribbling even faster. She could barely contain her enthusiasm, or her excitement to leave work.

"Does this have something to do with the Steller's sea cows?" the secretary asked in a hushed voice.

Geneva gave the secretary an exasperated look. The adventure of a lifetime was waiting for her, and all everyone wanted to do was waste her time asking questions! Questions she couldn't answer until she left and met Jase again, which would never happen at *this* rate.

Thank goodness Marnee had recovered, just as Jase had said. Geneva couldn't have left for The Sanctuary in clear conscience if the manatee's condition hadn't improved. Marnee had been admitted to the institute's intensive care unit, and Geneva had kept a round-the-clock vigil. It wasn't until Marnee was out of the woods that Geneva had definitely scheduled her present trip. Now, if only the staff would let her get to the airport!

Geneva took in a deep, calming breath. "Yes, my vacation has something to do with the Steller's sea cows," she replied honestly. "But I can't talk about it, other than to tell you I'll be staying in touch with the institute director." Did The Sanctuary have phones? Just what kind of place was she leaving for? "We wouldn't want the press to get hold of my location, now, would we?"

"Oh, so you're not *really* going to Bermuda, you're just *pretending* to go to Bermuda. I get it, Dr. Kelsey." The young secretary gave her a sly wink. "Say hi to the Eskimos for me."

"Inuit," Geneva automatically corrected her. She dropped the completed responses to the messages back on the desk. "Here. Do what you can with these. I'm going to lock up my office, then I'm outta here."

"But it's only eight-thirty, Dr. Kelsey! You have a meeting at ten, and—"

"Cancel it! I'm on vacation," Geneva firmly emphasized as she headed down the hall. *I've waited twenty years to find my brother. I'm not waiting a minute longer.*

She locked her office, hurried to the parking lot and took off for the airport in a rush. She'd already booked herself a flight on a Jacksonville-Miami shuttle. From there she would take a taxi to Miami's main pier and meet Jase.

Geneva impatiently counted the minutes until the plane touched down. Her luggage was a single carry-on bag, so she was able to head straight for the taxi section. Fortunately for her nerves, the ride to the pier was mercifully short. She was paying the driver when she heard her name.

"Hello, Geneva."

She whirled around to find Jase right behind her. The excitement that Geneva had felt all morning intensified into a burst of pleasure. "Jase! You're here!"

"I told you I would be." He reached over and took her bag from her, then watched the taxi leave before speaking again. "My boat's this way." He gestured for her to follow him toward one of the closer piers. "I understand Marnee's making a full recovery."

"Yes, she is…but Jase, how did you know?"

"I flew back to Jacksonville myself to check on her."

Geneva stopped dead in her tracks. "You didn't!"

"I did."

She felt a sudden pang inside that he'd been so close, yet had avoided her. "Why didn't you contact me?"

"You were busy. I didn't want to delay your departure with any more interruptions, but I wanted to make certain everything was all right with Marnee."

Geneva couldn't believe what she was hearing. Good lord, the trouble this man could get himself into! For once thoughts of Thomas didn't overshadow her concern for Jase himself. For a man she knew very little about, he was beginning to mean more to her than she'd realized.

"Jase, the last thing we need is security starting a file on you! You didn't pull your Dr. Doolittle thing in the hospital, did you?"

"And have them lock me up as some kind of nut case?" Jase shook his head and gave her that tiny mocking smile she now knew quite well. "No, Geneva, I do have more brains than that. Security didn't see me."

Geneva let out a sigh of relief. "Thank goodness."

Jase's expression was contemplative as he led her down the pier and placed her luggage on his boat. It wasn't until he reached for her hand to help her aboard that he spoke again.

"Don't tell me you were actually worried about me?"

Geneva hesitated, not wanting to tell him how much his welfare was beginning to occupy her thoughts. "Yes, I was. I mean, I owe you a lot," she said in confusion. "If it wasn't for your diagnosis, Marnee would be dead," she said in a rush of words. "She's going to be released back into the St. Johns River, thanks to you. I'm very grateful."

Jase helped her aboard the boat, then pulled her closer to him until their lips were inches apart. "*How* grateful, Geneva?"

There was no mistaking his meaning. His mouth claimed hers in a tender kiss that was feather light, yet was poised to deepen at the slightest encouragement from her.

Geneva was tempted—sorely tempted—to give him that encouragement, but thoughts of her brother intruded. Thomas had been kept within the confines of The Sanctuary by people exactly like Jase. True, Jase said Thomas had been treated well, but wasn't her twin still a bird in a gilded cage? A bird with clipped wings who could never go free? How could she allow herself to get involved with one of Thomas's captors?

Geneva was torn between her attraction to a man she hardly knew and the love for a twin she hadn't seen in twenty years. Despite the effect Jase's nearness had on her, she couldn't bring herself to go any further, not until she saw Thomas was all right. But neither could she bring herself to pull away....

Jase must have recognized her indecision, for he gently broke the kiss with a tolerant smile. "Conflicting loyalties, Geneva?" he asked quietly.

Geneva started at his sharp insight, then decided a lighthearted answer would be best. "I said I was grateful for what you did for Marnee, and I am. Are we ready to go?" she asked, deliberately changing the subject.

Jase continued to watch her. Just when Geneva thought she couldn't stand his assessing gaze any longer, he climbed to the captain's chair in the upraised flying bridge.

"As ready as we'll ever be. Why don't you stow your bag below while I fire up the engine?"

Geneva nodded. She went below, impressed by the plush interior of the boat. No expense had been spared; everything from the gold-plated faucets above the sink to the satin sheets on the berths looked brand-new. She cut short her explorations, however, when she heard the engine of the deep-hulled, forty-foot ocean craft spring into life.

"The cabins are downright luxurious. I'm impressed,'' Geneva said as she returned to the deck. "Whoever your travel agent is, I *definitely* want his name.''

"Sorry. He's for guardians only,'' Jase called down to her.

"I should have known,'' Geneva said ruefully, enjoying his amused glance.

"Ready to cast off?''

From the deck below, Geneva drew in a deep breath. *I'm as ready as I'll ever be.* She slipped the ropes off the moorings in response. "Casting off! She's all yours, Jase,'' Geneva called back.

Jase nodded, then waved her up to his side as he pulled away from the pier. Geneva took one last look at the safety of dry land and pushed aside any superstitious feelings. *She'd be seeing it again.*

Jase Guardian hadn't lied to her yet. Not once. As incredible as his statements had been, they'd all checked out so far. Maybe, just maybe, she'd actually see her brother again. And if Thomas was indeed happy and healthy, maybe she wouldn't feel so guilty about following up on the potent chemistry she felt around Jase.

"Come on up!'' Jase called to her as he slowly idled through the heavy marine traffic.

Conflicting loyalties or not, Geneva found herself eager to join him. She made a careful climb up the ladder to the flying bridge. Pumps and skirts were not the best clothes for a sea voyage, and she had more sensible items in her suitcase, but she had preferred not to wear them on the plane.

Jase held out his hand as she approached the top and drew her to his side before releasing her to place both hands back on the captain's wheel.

"It's a beautiful day to be out, isn't it?" Jase asked with a smile.

Geneva nodded. "Yes. I'm just glad you didn't end up spending yours in jail when you went to check on Marnee."

Jase turned her way, his gaze warm and welcoming. "You had nothing to worry about, Geneva, although I do appreciate your concern. I merely walked as close to the animal clinic as I could and talked to Marnee from there."

Geneva tilted her head in confusion, but was fascinated by his words. "You don't have to *see* the animal to talk to it?"

"Except for the initial contact, no, at least not with the higher life forms. That isn't true for the more primitive species. My range is very limited there."

"Oh." Geneva digested that fact. "I guess that makes sense. What's it like, Jase? Talking to them?"

"Sea creatures?" He considered that as he slung an arm around her shoulders. "Their thought processes are just like their swimming—graceful poetry in motion. For example, sirenians communicate slowly, like their body movements. Dolphins, however, are faster. Speed it up, sharpen it and add more beauty and harmony. Those are dolphins' thoughts. It varies from creature to creature."

"I wish... Oh, how I *wish* I could do what you do."

Jase's smile grew even larger. "Maybe you can. Many things are possible in The Sanctuary."

"Really?" Her eyes fired with eagerness. "But how could I... How do you..." Geneva broke off, and Jase finished the question for her.

"How do I do it?"

Geneva nodded.

"It's hard to explain, but it's kind of like seeing someone's expressions, then reading between the lines. Does that make sense?"

Nothing makes sense anymore. Especially you. Especially the way I'm feeling drawn toward you.

"I guess I'd have to experience it myself," she said. "I must admit to feeling a bit jealous."

Jase grinned and said nothing. Geneva was content to keep him company, and they enjoyed a companionable silence.

After a while she asked, "How long will it take us to get to The Sanctuary?"

"Let's see…" Geneva watched him study the setting summer sun. "It's 10:40 right now. We'll arrive some time before midnight. Longer if the seas are rough. We've got some big swells out today."

"How did you do that?" Geneva looked first for a watch on his wrist, then at the digital control panel for a chronometer. She saw neither.

"What? Predict the weather?"

"No. Tell the time correctly." She held out her own watch for him to see.

"Oh, that." Jase shrugged. "I can tell just by looking at the sun and its relative position over the sea's horizon."

"What if it's dark?"

"If it's dark, I can always use the stars. If worse comes to worst, I can feel the tides and calculate from there using the moon, but that takes a bit longer. Not much, though."

"You can *feel* the tides?"

"Yep."

"And just where do you feel them?" she asked curiously, watching his bronze hands skillfully steer the boat out toward open ocean.

"In my soul." At her soft intake of air, he took his gaze off his piloting duties for just a second, his blue eyes intense. "Not very scientific, is it?"

"Hey, if it works…" Geneva managed to reply.

"It works," he assured her, returning to his duties. Even this late in the day, the recreational boat traffic around Miami was still heavy.

Geneva watched as Jase kicked his feet out of his shoes, then started to unbutton his shirt. She couldn't seem to keep her eyes off him. His body was just as appealing to her as his personality, and the seductive aura of mystery he wore. But right now, it was his perfectly sculpted body that was making her pulse quicken. Finally he was free of everything except his jeans.

Geneva swallowed hard, feeling relief—or was it regret?—that he hadn't kissed her while half-dressed like this. She would never have been able to draw away so easily if he had. Geneva silently decided it would be wisest to stay uninvolved, at least until she saw Thomas. Until then, it would be hands off, for *both* of them.

"You don't like clothes much, do you?" she asked, holding on to the bridge railing against the rocking of the boat and pretending a casualness she was far from feeling.

"Not new ones, anyway. A woman isn't the only thing I've gone without lately."

"Dr. Doolittle joins a nudist colony?" Geneva asked with curiosity—and a totally unexpected, wanton rush of desire. Obviously her traitorous body and vivid imagination was going to make it very difficult to hold fast to her newly made resolution.

Holding one arm upright, his palm facing her, Jase said, "I solemnly swear to wear spandex for the duration of your visit."

"*I* certainly intend to," Geneva retorted. It was best to be sensible and set things straight right now. "I don't feel like parading around naked in front of the rest of your guardians."

"You can please yourself on that score, Geneva. No one else will see you."

"But..." Geneva felt that unexpected rush of desire escalate to fever pitch. "Why not?"

"I'm the only guardian on my island. There will only be you, me and my marine wards. No one else."

There was silence on the boat. Then Geneva spoke. "The two of us alone on a deserted island?"

Jase's eyes danced wildly. "Consider it an unexpected bonus to our...business agreement."

"Business agreement?" Geneva echoed harshly. Suddenly business was the furthest thing from her mind.

"That's right. You give us the sea cows, and we give you your brother. Strictly business. And The Sanctuary always keeps its bargains."

"Why do I get the feeling that you're *not* going to act like a perfect gentleman?"

Jase turned his attention away from the sea and focused it fully on her. "Why do I get the feeling that you don't want me to?" he countered. The hunger in his eyes was clearly visible.

"I never said that!" Geneva took an involuntary step backward, but Jase reached for her and pulled her close until they were mere inches apart.

"Maybe not with words, but you've said it just the same."

Geneva flushed. She *had* been sending him mixed messages. If it wasn't for Thomas, there'd be no doubt as to what message she'd be sending him.

"Listen carefully, Geneva. You're a beautiful woman, we're going to be totally alone on my island, and God knows I'm only human."

He pulled her even closer, and Geneva's hands splayed against his bare chest at his sudden motion. She could smell the salty scent of his skin, could feel the tension in the muscles beneath her fingers. Despite her best intentions, she couldn't help but be affected by Jase's potent brand of magic. Her lips leaned toward his, but this time it was Jase who held back.

"Don't start anything you don't intend to finish, Geneva." He lifted one hand from her arm and gently tucked a stray strand of hair back behind her ear. "Because if you change your mind midstream, I don't know if I could stop."

Those words shocked her out of whatever thrall he'd held her in. Geneva realized she was holding her breath and slowly let it out. "Fair enough."

His eyes narrowed. "Don't be so glib. And don't underestimate your effect on me, Geneva. I'm serious."

"So am I." She lifted her chin, determined to be honest. "I'm no shrinking violet, Jase. I'm a damn good biologist who knows all about wants and needs, especially since the only satisfying partner I've ever had in my life is my work. Believe me, there's too much at stake for me to play Brooke Shields at the *Blue Lagoon*."

Jase's lips twitched upward, and he guided her back

to his side before placing his hands back on the pilot's wheel. Geneva felt strangely bereft without his touch.

"So now I've gone from being Dr. Doolittle to Christopher Atkins?"

"Hardly," Geneva replied, more than a little chagrined. "You can tell my social life's in the dumps. I watch a lot of TV at night."

"With your briefcase and microwave dinners, of course."

"Of course," Geneva admitted lightly. "Life in the slow lane, that's me."

"I haven't watched TV for years. Believe it or not, I still miss it sometimes."

"You don't have television on the island?"

"No. Just radio."

"Oh." Geneva watched his long brown hair blow in the ocean breeze, glad that hers was braided, yet enjoying the freedom of his. "What was your favorite show?"

"Don't laugh," he warned.

"I won't."

"I loved watching the Road Runner on Saturdays."

Geneva couldn't hide her amusement. "Cartoons? For a grown man?"

"*And* the Boston Red Sox," he said defensively.

"Quite a combination—baseball bats and falling anvils."

"Well, the Coyote always made me laugh." Geneva heard the wistful tone in his voice that disappeared as he asked, "What's your favorite show?"

"Oh, definitely Oprah. I always tape her programs, even the reruns."

"Who's Oprah?"

"Who's Oprah?" Geneva was flabbergasted. "*Everyone* knows Oprah!"

Jase shrugged. "I don't."

"How could you *not?* She's a famous talk-show hostess who discusses all kinds of interesting, controversial, trendy subjects with various people."

"I'll pass. I have enough interesting, controversial subjects in my own life." He gave her a pointed glance. "Don't you?"

"I suppose…" Geneva concentrated on the ocean before her, hoping the sounds of the sea would calm her suddenly overactive sexuality that always seemed to spring into action around Jase Guardian.

"You should go change out of your work clothes before it gets much darker," Jase suggested after a while. "Did you bring a jacket? It gets cold once the sun goes down."

"I brought one." She headed down the ladder.

"Do you have everything you need for the next few days?"

"I'm all set." Geneva reached the main deck.

"There are no drugstores where we're going," he warned. "If you need any toothpaste or medicine, it's too far to go back to Miami. And The Sanctuary's selection is rather limited."

"I do know how to pack a tube of toothpaste, Jase. And I have some aspirin just in case."

"No medical problems?" There was a curious note to his voice. Concern, and something else…

"None." Geneva was touched by his consideration.

"No allergies? I have stinging insects on my island."

"No allergies, not even to pollen. I'm as healthy as a horse."

Jase nodded his satisfaction. "I don't want anything to happen to you. I want you back home again without a scratch."

"Thank you for asking, Jase." She gave him a tremulous smile. "No one's made a fuss over me since my parents disappeared. That's why I'm so eager to see Thomas again. My aunts and uncles have been good to me, but I've really missed my own family." She gave him a curious look. "Jase, I know you said you didn't have a wife. Don't you have any family at all?"

"I have no commitments. I thought there was no place for those in The Sanctuary. But lately, I've decided that I may have been mistaken."

Geneva felt a vast sense of relief. So even though he wasn't committed to anyone, he didn't have anything against family. Somehow she knew she would have hated it if his answer had been different. Jase's voice intruded into her thoughts.

"It's getting dark, Geneva. Go below and come back up after you've changed. And be careful climbing down that ladder in those shoes."

Geneva gave him a thumbs-up. As she changed in her own private berth, she tried to imagine Jase in the real world sitting around the house watching baseball. It was hard to picture. He just didn't fit the mold of an everyday, ordinary kind of guy. She wondered what he'd been like in his previous, pre-Sanctuary existence. Did he really laugh at cartoons in another lifetime?

Geneva reached into her suitcase for some long pants and a sweater, her expression pensive. Despite Jase's smiles and occasional bursts of amusement, she knew now he was no longer the man he once had been.

And that the reason for his hermitlike existence on a lonely island in a forbidden sea must have been powerful. But was it powerful enough to forbid Geneva Kelsey from being a part of his life, even if it was only for a short time?

She wondered if he'd ever tell her about it, then found herself hoping that he would. The subject of Jase Guardian had suddenly become very intriguing, in more ways than one....

The sun had completely set when Geneva climbed topside again.

"Don't you ever get cold?" she asked Jase as she rejoined him, noticing that his shirt and shoes were still lying where he'd discarded them. There was a distinct chill to the air that she could feel even through her cable-knit pullover.

"Of course I do. I've simply built up more of a tolerance to the elements since I left behind heated houses and air-conditioned cars." He raised one eyebrow. "What did you think, Geneva? That I'm some comic-book hero with super powers?"

"No. Well, maybe..." she admitted sheepishly.

Jase smiled. "Superman I'm not. I eat, sleep and bleed just like the next guy. And in case you're wondering, no, I don't have gills. I can't breathe underwater. When necessary, I use scuba gear when I work, just like you."

"But you do have certain gifts, Jase. I've seen them! You *aren't* like other men. You're much more..." *Enticing,* Geneva thought. "...powerful than the average man. You can't deny that. What I'd like to know is, why you?"

Jase turned on the boat's running lights in the growing twilight before replying. Geneva sat down on half of the spacious captain's chair. Jase, who had been standing, sat down also, his hands still on the large wooden ship's wheel. Geneva could feel the warmth from his body as his thigh and shoulder touched hers.

"The Sanctuary gives different powers to different people," Jase said slowly. "Those powers are random and totally unpredictable. Supposedly our personalities and intellect have something to do with it." He shrugged. "I've never been able to figure out that part of it myself. Suffice to say that, although I do have certain unusual abilities, my gifts are limited."

"Gifts? As in plural? You can do *more* than communicate with marine life?"

"I can not only communicate with them, I can also command their loyalty."

And mine, Geneva found herself thinking. Whatever magic Jase had, it was also working on her. And his magic was powerful indeed. She'd had a hard time resisting his wishes—*him*—since the first day she'd seen him.

Jase nodded. "And a few other things."

"Such as?" Heavens, trying to get words out of Jase Guardian was like prying pearls from oysters. "Tell me, Jase."

"Well," he said after careful consideration, "in addition to communicating with sea life, I can come and go safely in any ocean on this planet, at any time of the year, under any conditions. I can also travel those same oceans without any navigational instruments. All I need is my eyes. Sometimes I don't even need those. With a few minor exceptions, that's it, Geneva."

"That's *it?*" Geneva echoed. "Jase Guardian, that's more than just *it!* That's incredible!"

"If you're wise, you won't envy us our Sanctuary

powers. Many of us paid dearly for them. And then some.''

"And you, Jase? Are you one of those who paid dearly?" Geneva asked curiously.

Jase smiled his tiny, mocking smile and said nothing.

Geneva closed her mouth with frustration. She was falling fast for a mystery man: a man whose personal life still remained distinctly off limits. Being attracted to a stranger was one thing. Becoming involved with a man who insisted on remaining a stranger was downright dangerous. Then and there Geneva resolved to find out who Jase Guardian was—with or without his help.

She remained quiet for a long while. Time passed as she watched the lights of Miami finally fade off in the distance.

"I like my berth," she said after the silence grew uncomfortable. "Is this your boat?"

"It's mine to use as long as I remain a guardian."

"Am I allowed to ask how long?"

"Yes, but I don't know the answer to that." Jase ran one hand over the back of his neck, then returned it to the pilot's wheel. "As long as I want, I suppose. I've never heard of anyone leaving for good once they've sworn their loyalty to The Sanctuary."

"But it's permitted?"

"Oh, yes. Many guardians have family in the real world that they visit from time to time."

"But you don't. Jase, I think that's so sad." And suddenly, the words came tumbling out. "You could come and visit me, if you want. You know, like for the holidays or something."

Geneva had the feeling she'd caught him off guard.

He turned and stared at her at first, and didn't say a word.

"It's an open invitation," she said, embarrassed at what seemed to be his negative reaction. "I didn't mean to put you on the spot."

"You haven't. You just caught me by surprise, that's all."

"Then you don't think it's a bad idea?"

Jase gave her a brushing kiss on the cheek. "I think it's a very generous offer. I don't get many invitations where I'm from."

Geneva basked under his praise—and his touch. Suddenly the night was a precious thing to be enjoyed again. She smiled at him, enjoying his nearness, enjoying the intimate look he returned. Instead of two people from different worlds, they could be any couple on a romantic twilight cruise. Geneva shivered with delight at that fantasy.

Jase immediately put his arm around her shoulders. "Cold?"

She lifted her face to his. "I'm just fine." And with him there, she was, but Jase didn't take her at her word.

"I've got a thermos of coffee down on the deck. Why don't I set the boat on automatic pilot? There's little traffic out here. We can go stretch our legs."

Geneva hated giving up her cozy seat next to him, but remembering her earlier vow to remain uninvolved until she saw Thomas again, she good-naturedly followed his suggestion. Jase poured her coffee into the single thermos cup, then stood next to her on the railing, the moonlight and the running lights softly illuminating his tall frame.

"You drink first. I'll have mine when you're done,"

Jase said. "Would you like some sugar packets or cream? I can run down to the galley for you."

"Black is fine." Especially since she didn't want to lose Jase's company again. She lifted the thermos cup and took an appreciative sip. "Thank you, Jase."

"You're very welcome."

Geneva leaned against the railing at the bow of the ship. The breeze caressed her cheeks, the calm night air soothed her. She sighed with contentment.

"Tired, Geneva?"

She shook her head. "Oh, no. Just the opposite. If it wasn't for the fog up ahead, I'd almost hate for this trip to end." She turned away from the ocean to watch him again. "How much farther?" she asked, wiping a few droplets of salt spray from her cheeks.

"Not much."

"Good." Geneva drank more coffee. "It's getting foggy out here. I don't mind the dark, but this stuff—" She gestured at the heavy banks. "I'd hate to be lost in this mess."

Jase leaned against the railing himself, his bare feet spread wide against the slight rolling of the deck, his chest glistening with moisture. "You wouldn't be the first."

Geneva looked out toward the ocean again and was bewitched by the sight. Everywhere the fog was rolling in faster and thicker than she'd ever seen before— and Geneva was no stranger to these waters. The ocean was glowing with a strange luminescence, the waters crisscrossed with streaks of green-blue light she'd never witnessed before. They had an eerie radiance all their own.

"Shouldn't you be getting back to the bridge?" she asked suddenly. Despite its haunting beauty, the sea was looking more foreign, more unearthly by the minute. It certainly wasn't the kind of sea favored for easy navigation.

"Don't worry, Geneva. I never get lost. Besides, my escorts are here."

"Escorts?"

"My wards."

"Where?" Even with the running lights, Geneva could barely see him nod in the growing haze.

"Turn around again and see."

Geneva finished the last of her coffee in one great gulp, stowed the cup in a deck chest and rejoined him at the bow of the boat. Lightning flashed as it shot across the clouds directly overhead. In its light, Geneva saw the school of porpoises, their glistening, leaping bodies illuminated. Even as she admired their wild beauty, she tensed in anticipation for the crack of thunder.

The crack of thunder that should have followed never came.

Geneva lifted wide eyes to Jase and spoke, wondering if she'd even hear the sound of her own voice. "I'm not going deaf, am I? I did just see lightning."

"Your ears aren't playing tricks on you, Geneva. There's no thunder here at the barriers."

"No thunder?" As if to underscore her words, another silent flash flickered overhead. "I don't think I like this place," she said clearly.

Jase laughed, but it wasn't a pleasant sound. A chill went down her spine as he said, "Very few do, Geneva. Very few do."

The fog rolled in even closer as the soundless lightning continued to flash overhead. The wind picked up until it howled its fury and whitecaps frothed, but the sea was still relatively calm. Despite the relative steadiness of the deck, Geneva felt dizzy; she suddenly swayed. Jase was at her side in an instant, his arms around her waist as he supported her tightly against his chest. She grabbed at his shoulders, her eyes apologizing for her momentary weakness, even as she willingly drew on his strength.

"I'm so dizzy, Jase. I've never lost my sea legs before," she said breathlessly. "Is this caused by The Sanctuary? Or you?"

Jase leaned even closer, his sea-blue eyes locked with hers. "Let's find out, shall we?"

And he brought his mouth down hard on hers. His lips demanded a response—a response Geneva was only too willing to make. The deck seemed to tilt wildly beneath her feet; the man holding her was the only stable thing in her surreal world. He wove a spell of seduction with his touch, first enticing, then demanding, until a trembling Geneva was kissing him back with every ounce of strength, every ounce of passion, she had.

It was more than just The Sanctuary that was magic. It was more than just The Sanctuary's man that was magic. It was the two of them together that was overpoweringly enchanted.

So overpowering that a paralyzing weakness spread through her body.

"Jase? Jase?" she cried, knowing something was wrong, but not understanding what was happening.

"Don't be frightened. I drugged your coffee, Geneva."

"You drugged me?" Geneva fought against the deadly lethargy coursing through her veins. "Why?"

"Because, my sweet, strangers who learn the way into The Sanctuary are never allowed to leave."

Geneva's head lolled back, her eyes still open. She felt one of his hands slide up her spine to support her limp neck. Frantically she tried to make sense of this mystical place where the normal laws of nature didn't apply. She failed miserably, as did her strength.

Jase gently brought her head forward again. "You don't want to stay here forever, now, do you, Geneva Kelsey?"

Geneva didn't know how to answer that. Overhead the noiseless lightning flashed and flashed over and over again while the porpoises at the bow leapt in flight.

I don't know what I want, Geneva thought as she trembled in his arms.

Her last conscious memory was of Jase's lips on hers again and his deep voice in her ears as he answered his own question.

"I didn't think so."

Chapter Six

My mate? You want to know if the woman is my mate?

Jase blinked at the question from his dolphins as he felt for a pulse in the slim wrist of the woman in the hammock. It was sluggish, but beat with healthy strength.

You want to see her? You want to see us both?

He gently replaced Geneva's arm at her side and adjusted the light blanket he'd covered her with the previous night, all the while listening to the excited chatter of his wards in the lagoon.

I can't come out yet. No, the woman—he hesitated to use the term ''mate'' that his dolphins had labeled her with, even though the term strongly appealed to him—*can't come swim with you, either. She's still sleeping. Later! Later, later, later...*

He kept sending the message until the dolphins finally accepted his answer. But he could feel their waiting excitement and impatience in his mind, bubbling below the surface of his own consciousness. Jase was surprised at their uncharacteristic insistence. They were so very eager to meet ''the mate'' of their guardian.

Jase was even more surprised at the train of thought

his dolphins had sparked. What *was* Geneva Kelsey to him? Long ago he'd stopped thinking of her as just a business partner. And somewhere along the line he'd stopped viewing her as just any woman. He'd started to think of her as a *special* woman.... Maybe as someone who *could* be his mate.

Even if they were from different worlds. Even if they could only be together for a very short time, time he was wasting by sitting here letting her sleep.

Suddenly he was a little impatient himself. Without medical intervention, Geneva wasn't due to wake up any time soon. The potent dosage Jase had given her had made certain of that. He'd originally planned on letting her sleep it off.

But the dolphins and other marine animals were hounding him unmercifully. Even now they were assaulting his senses with their urgency. His wards wanted him—and Geneva—in the water. He'd been gone from The Sanctuary for too long, they insisted. They missed him. They loved him. They wanted to see him. *Now.*

All right, you win, he said with a paternal burst of affection. *I'll wake her up, but only if you promise to stop pestering me until we come out.*

Delighted consents filled his head. Only after they dwindled down to a more bearable level did Jase leave his vigil in the screen-enclosed patio that served as the sleeping area. He headed straight for the antidote locked inside his desk.

Jase prepared the hypodermic, then swabbed her limp arm. He fought against a strong reluctance to puncture that soft, silky skin, hated to jab the needle directly into her vein. But his wards sent him soothing reassurance, and he was able to slowly empty the syringe.

"That ought to do the trick," he said to himself, withdrawing the needle and holding a cotton ball over the tiny red hole. A few minutes of direct pressure, a few more to let the antidote work, and Geneva Kelsey would be back among the land of the living.

Jase once more adjusted her blanket before locking the antidote back in his desk. Geneva's eyes were just starting to flutter open as he pulled up a wicker stool and positioned himself next to the hammock where she could see him.

"Hello, Geneva." He didn't touch her, didn't want to frighten her, for her disorientation was readily apparent.

"Jase?" Her voice was even softer than usual, her words velvety with sleep instead of hoarse.

"Yes. You're on my island."

A rush of memory crossed her face. "You kissed me!" Geneva suddenly remembered.

Jase gave her a slow, satisfied smile. "I drugged your coffee, too. Or did my kiss make you forget that?"

Geneva frowned, annoyed at him for that totally male look of smugness. And annoyed at herself for letting her attraction to him overrule her vow to concentrate on Thomas, not Jase.

"How could I forget that?" Geneva shot him an annoyed look. "Do you always go around drugging strange women?"

"Only those whose futures I care about. I'm sorry, Geneva, but it was for your own protection. I couldn't let you learn the way in here. If you had, I wouldn't be allowed to take you home again."

Geneva licked her lips. They were dry, but she didn't know if that was a medical side effect, or if it had something to do with Jase's nearness. Waking up to find a man's bare chest just inches away from her sleepy body was somewhat disconcerting, yet strangely exciting. It hinted of intimacies she found herself wanting to follow up on. But she didn't dare…at least, not yet. She had her priorities, and she intended to stick to them, no matter how difficult it might be.

"I'm in The Sanctuary now?" Geneva waited for confirmation.

"Yes."

She immediately strained to sit up. "I want to see my brother," she demanded, her voice stronger now.

"Don't do that!" Jase pressed her shoulders back into the soft woven cotton of the hammock. "Give yourself a few minutes yet. The antidote can cause unpleasant side effects if you don't remain quiet."

Geneva struggled against him with surprising strength. "I want to see Thomas *now!*" She kicked her feet and tilted the hammock enough so that she was dumped into his arms. They both sank to the ground, Jase on his knees, Geneva's limbs a cross-legged tangle.

Geneva felt Jase grab at her. "Geneva, please, you're going to make yourself sick."

Geneva clutched at him as a wave of dizziness attacked. "The room is spinning," she gasped.

He scooped her up in his arms and held her very, very still. Geneva allowed herself to relax in his arms. It wasn't hard; his nearness always affected her more than she would let on. She didn't even resist as he smoothed back her tangled black hair. But when she felt her own pulse quicken at his caresses, she steeled her heart and pushed away his hand.

"Don't do that. Where's Thomas?"

Jase showed no reaction to her rejection, she noticed with a sudden pang. "Your brother's not on this island," he said. "Even if he was, you're in no shape to see him today. You need some food and fresh air to clear your head first."

"And a drink," she said, her lips still dry.

"No drinks yet. It'll make you sick to your stomach. Trust me, the antidote packs quite a wallop. The dizziness will pass shortly if you lie still."

So Geneva lay still.

"Geneva…"

"What?" she replied, looking up at him and trying hard to pretend that the feel of his bare chest under her cheek meant nothing.

"Do you like coconut?"

"Coconut?" She lifted her head up from the cradle of his arm to stare at him.

"I have some fresh stuff. If you want, you could chew on a piece."

"Chew?"

"Yeah. You know. To get the cotton taste out of your mouth."

Geneva suddenly smiled. "I'd be your pal for life."

Jase took in the tousled black hair, the dusky rose of her lips and the amusement in her eyes. After all she'd been through, she could still smile. Amazing.

"For a pretty lady, you sure come cheap. I'll bring you some, but let me get you back into the hammock." Jase gently lifted her and did exactly that. And then, silently cursing the irony of one beautiful, sleepy-eyed *pal* lying chastely in his hammock, he hurried to the kitchen.

Within an hour, Geneva was much improved. Jase saw the color return to her cheeks and the grogginess of a chemical hangover disappear.

"You look much better," he observed.

"I feel better. I'd like to clean up." She sat up, the hammock swinging as her bare feet swung over the side. Geneva grimaced at the wrinkled appearance of the slacks and blouse she'd worn the night before. "And change."

"I put your suitcase in the hall by the bathroom. Your shoes and sweater are there, too." He held out his hand to help her out of the hammock, and after a moment, she took it.

"You're not dizzy anymore, are you?"

"Not a bit."

"Then I'll give you the nickel tour." Jase reluctantly released her fingers the moment she pulled away from him. "This porch is the sleeping area. I'll sling you up a hammock later. I don't have any bedrooms. Or beds. Straight through here is the living area. Follow me."

Jase watched as Geneva carefully took in her surroundings. "Electric lights *and* oil lamps?" she said, observing his desk.

"I have a solar-powered setup, which is useless during the winter storms. The oil lamps come in handy."

Geneva nodded and turned her attention toward the far northern wall. "Look at all these books!" She hurried over to the floor-to-ceiling shelves where his extensive array of both fiction and nonfiction was stored. Her eyes scanned the titles.

"I read a lot," Jase replied, watching her gently run her fingers over the spines of his books.

"So I see. This is quite an impressive collection. The marine biology section alone is as good as that at the institute."

Jase enjoyed her obvious pleasure. "Thank you. Feel free to help yourself anytime. I'm afraid you won't be watching much 'Oprah' here." He was pleased that he'd remembered the name of her favorite show, pleased even more that she smiled. He waited for a few more seconds, then said, "The kitchen is right off the living area. I have an old-fashioned cooler, but I don't use it much. Mostly I catch my meals on the spot."

"I would have thought you'd be a vegetarian."

Jase shrugged. "I would, if the situation warranted, but it's not necessary. I don't eat the endangered species, of course, or any of the higher life forms. But this *is* a preserve. Space is limited. We can't allow any one population to overstep what The Sanctuary can comfortably support, so guardians are allowed to harvest wisely, just as the predator fish harvest their prey. I do have a garden to supplement the seafood, and there are all the tropical fruit trees."

"I'd love to see them," Geneva said, looking out of one of the many screened windows in Jase's home. "And your sea creatures."

"The bathroom's right behind the kitchen. Go change, then I'll take you outside. You can't go alone, not at first."

Geneva nodded. She was changed and back at Jase's side faster than he thought possible.

"That was quick," he observed. Geneva saw him take in her pale green one-piece suit with the matching wraparound skirt. "Do you have any sandals? The beach can get really hot if you aren't used to going barefoot."

"I only wear shoes in my office and when I'm back in Alaska."

"Maybe you should take a hat," he suggested. "That Alaskan half of you might burn."

"The Spanish half never does. Let's go."

She hurried outside into the path among the mango and papaya trees. Despite her enthusiasm to see what kind of a world Thomas inhabited, she waited for Jase. He took her hand in his, but allowed her to set the pace down to the lagoon at the bottom of the sandy hill where his bungalow sat.

"Jase!" Geneva stopped in amazement, her hands flying to her cheeks. "Look at all the turtles!"

"In all The Sanctuary, my beach is their favorite." Jase urged her forward with a hand on the small of her back, for she was still rooted to the spot.

"But there must be hundreds of them! I've never seen so many in one place!"

"That's because most beaches are trampled by humans."

"Or because they love you?" she softly asked. "Look at them, Jase!" Geneva watched as many of the turtles immediately made straight for Jase, their determination to reach him obvious in their hurried motions. She stared at him in awe. As more and more turtles reached the path and clustered around his feet, Jase Guardian looked more in his element than ever.

"That, too," he said with a smile. Geneva watched as he bent and gently stroked the heads of the nearest specimens.

Geneva remained where she was, not wanting to

move for fear of injuring the creatures covering the path.

"Do they always come to you like this?" she asked in awe.

"Well, they are supposed to stay off my path, but since you're on my island, their curiosity is getting the better of them." Jase straightened up and gave her an unfathomable look. "They think you're my new mate, you know."

"Your…mate?" Geneva swayed as her wayward mind conjured up wanton images, then started as Jase grabbed her arm.

"You okay?"

"Umm, yes," she said on a shaky note. "It's hard to walk with all your turtles around," she fibbed, still unsettled by the thought of herself as Jason's "mate."

Jase gave her a long, assessing look. Geneva had the feeling she hadn't fooled him one bit.

"I'll have my wards clear the path," he finally said as he steered her around them. "Careful. These are nesting sands on either side of us. When you want to reach the lagoon, always remember to stay on this path."

"I will." Geneva nodded, watching the mass exodus of turtles start as quickly as their arrival had begun. How in the world did he *do* that? She felt the continuing pressure of his hand on her arm as they finally reached the lagoon.

"Jase, what kind of turtle is that?"

"Which one?"

"The large one in the water." She pointed off in the distance, causing his arm to fall away. "I recognized the leatherbacks and the greens, and of course the hawksbill and loggerheads. But that particular species..." She shook her head. "I'm embarrassed to admit that I can't come close to identifying it. I've never seen one before."

"Very few people have. That particular turtle is a favorite of mine. Let's go down to the water and I'll call her for you."

They crossed the hot sands and waded into ankle-deep water.

Come on in, my dear. I want you to meet someone.

At his command, the sea turtle headed toward the shallower waters.

"Jase, I can't believe the size!" Geneva cried out as the turtle edged in closer. "It's huge!"

Jase smiled. "Only ten feet from head to tail, and a mere eighteen-hundred kilograms."

"Almost two tons?"

Geneva untied her skirt, threw it onto the sand and waded thigh-deep. Jase found his attention immediately drawn to her slim, curving legs and the enticing sway of her hips.

"I know I'm a marine biologist, and I definitely feel like a fool for asking, but *what* in the world is it?"

"She's an Archelon."

"An Arch— But they're extinct! All we have is fossils of them."

Jase smiled. "We have more than that here, Geneva."

"Every book I've read says Archelon sea turtles went out in prehistoric times with the T-rex and the stegosaurus!" Geneva continued to stare at the giant reptile.

"Susie's been laying eggs in this lagoon as long as I can remember."

"Susie?" Geneva's eyes flicked from the turtle to him. "Is that her name?"

"It's *my* name for her. Turtles don't name themselves like the cetaceans do. They identify each other by shell markings."

Geneva studied the unusual shell markings on the green-brown back as the turtle glided by. "How old is this specimen—this Susie?" she corrected herself.

"At least eighty years old. Her mate is older, but he's…" Jase concentrated on the male Archelon, his eyes narrowing with the effort. "He's feeding out in the deeper waters."

"And you can actually tell that just by thinking?"

"Yes."

Geneva shook her head in astonishment. The fact that Jase could actually talk to turtles was just as amazing as the prehistoric turtle itself. Maybe more so…

"She's beautiful, Jase." Geneva extended her hand as the Archelon floated closer. "Can I touch her?"

Jase grabbed her arm. "No, don't!"

He held her hand tightly against his chest, safely away from the turtle's beak. Geneva stopped trying to reach for the turtle. Her fingers involuntarily splayed gently over his skin, meshing themselves in the curling hair on his chest. It was with the greatest difficulty she refrained from doing the same with her other hand.

"Archelons can be quite aggressive. I'm safe, because the creatures here in The Sanctuary won't harm guardians. You're *not* a guardian, and they know that."

"Oh."

Jase gently released her fingers, but Geneva left her

hand where it was. "In other words, I need you to baby-sit me?"

"More like escort you." Jase put both hands on her shoulders and turned her to face him. "Geneva, listen carefully. I care for many creatures that you've never studied, let alone seen. Some of them are quite fragile. Others, like my almost-extinct American crocodiles, are quite dangerous. Most, like the Archelons, are quite rare. For both your protection and theirs, Geneva, you must be very, very careful. And follow my instructions to the letter."

"I will." Geneva sighed. His touch was potent enough to distract her from thoughts of everything except Jase, yet all he'd wanted to do was give her a lecture in conservation. Was the attraction she felt toward him strictly one-sided? She watched quietly as Susie swam away, then stepped away herself until his hands fell from her shoulders.

"I should know better, working with manatees. I promise just to look, not touch."

"I have plenty of other sea creatures here I can show you," Jase reassured her. "Creatures you *can* touch. Would you like to see my dolphins?"

"Oh, yes!" Geneva's eyes, which had momentarily dulled, sparkled again.

"Which breed would you like to see?" he asked with a smile. To her delight, he reached for her hand again and held it closely within his. Geneva didn't pull away this time.

"Any breed is fine, Jase, but I don't see anything."

"They all retreated at the first hint of a nonguardian in their lagoon, but they'll come back if I call. Any species will."

Geneva gazed up at him, marveling at his words. "Any?"

"Yes, although the Commerson and bottle-nose dolphins have formed a particular attachment to me. They're never far away. But you might be more interested in the seriously endangered species. I can show you the Hector's dolphin, the Indo-Pacific and Atlantic humpbacked dolphins, the Franciscana and Baiji, or the Vaquita."

"You have all of those here, Jase?" Geneva's eyes swept across the lagoon, looking for the distinctive leaping dolphin fins, but seeing nothing yet.

"All the ocean-dwelling species, yes. I don't have the freshwater species. The three endangered freshwater dolphins are on one of our larger islands that has a major river system."

"Do you get to see them?" Geneva asked curiously.

"No. The Indus and Ganges River dolphins, and the Yangtze River's Baiji dolphins are in the care of another guardian."

"I'm amazed. They're so very rare."

"They're rare here, too. We don't have many. In The Sanctuary, fresh water is at a premium. Still, we do maintain a healthy breeding population."

Geneva nodded. "I'm glad to hear it, considering freshwater dolphins number in the mere hundreds."

"So do some of the saltwater dolphins. At last count, there were only a few hundred Vaquitas in the Gulf of California. But my favorite has always been the bottle-nose dolphin. Even before I could communicate with them, I was crazy about them."

"You've worked with them before?" Geneva immediately asked.

For just a moment, Jase remembered the old days

of his clinic and how he'd failed his very first wards. A chill swept through him, and his free hand clenched involuntarily into a fist. "It was a long time ago," he said, unaware of the anguish in his eyes. "Another lifetime…"

Geneva's own eyes were wide and sympathetic. It was that tender concern, that comforting squeeze she made with her fingers over his, that enabled Jase to shove those painful memories aside. He mentally braced himself for more questions. Or worse yet, her pity.

Instead, Geneva gave him a lovely smile, a smile that was filled with compassion and understanding. "I like bottle-nose, too," she said simply.

Jase's mouth parted in amazement.

"I'd love to see them," she added. She released his hand to wade deeper into the water, and for a second Jase felt starkly alone. But then she lifted her face to his with an air of expectation—and trust. "I'm ready whenever you are."

For the first time since the clinic's destruction, Jase felt a strength within that he thought HADES had destroyed. Her faith in him touched something he thought was long dead. He felt honored, proud, and most of all secure in the knowledge that her trust was not misplaced.

Impulsively he bent down and kissed her cheek. And then, because he felt much more than gratitude, he kissed her again full on the mouth. His lips held hers captive. He couldn't bear to let her go—not while her response was so honest, so sweet…so incredibly exciting. It wasn't until Geneva drew back herself that Jase allowed the kiss to end. He looped his arm around her waist, his face inches from hers, and strode deeper into the crystalline waters of his lagoon.

"Come on, my Sweet Survivor. You want dolphins?"

She nodded, her face alive with excitement—an excitement that traveled from her soft body to his. He felt the foreign, long-forgotten sensation of life, of joy, of exhilaration, bubbling up deep inside. And the former Dr. Jason Merrick couldn't help but yield to the experience.

"Then I'll give you dolphins."

Jase closed his eyes and sent his mind to every far-reaching depth of his territory. Then he sent it even further until his command reached each and every barrier of The Sanctuary. And with the overwhelming speed of creatures at one with the sea, the dolphins and porpoises came.

And came. *And came.*

He heard Geneva gasp as the waters of the lagoon quickly filled with a riot of flashing colors. White, black, spotted, gray, brown, humped and smooth, large and small…all gathered in the lagoon. Soon the waters were frothing with the riotous exuberance of dolphins.

But Jase didn't watch the dolphins. He watched Geneva's lips as they parted in amazement, Geneva's hands as they flew to her mouth, Geneva's expression of silent wonder as her eyes met his, then flew back to the creatures all heading toward them, each smooth body avoiding the others in a vibrant, adept dance.

The smaller dolphins and porpoises came up close and surrounded them in the waist-deep water. The squeaks and squeals were overwhelming, the sonar transmissions speeding through the waters and crashing in a deafening cascade in Jase's mind. He toned it down, all the while concentrating on Geneva.

Her hands dropped from her mouth and fanned through the water, her eagerness to touch the dolphins evident. Jase saw her desire and granted it.

She won't hurt you. She's a friend. Let her touch you. She's safe, you're safe, we're all safe.

And in a solid, synchronized motion, the whirling circular dance of the dolphins closed in on them.

And touched her.

Geneva let out a cry of surprise as the first speeding dolphin grazed against her leg. She started and almost lost her balance in the sandy bottom and the churning waters. The delicate sonar of a good twenty dolphins immediately made lightning-quick fin and tail adjustments to avoid collision as Jase steadied her.

He started to speak, to reassure her not to be frightened. But Geneva wasn't frightened. To Jase's amazement, she was laughing!

Her head was thrown back, her mouth wide and joyous. And every time another dolphin grazed her hand or arm or leg, another peal of laughter erupted. When one dolphin boldly leapt high over their heads, raining seawater on Geneva's ebony hair, she clapped her hands like an enraptured child. Jase thought he'd never seen anything so beautiful in his life.

Her laughter dwindled and was replaced by a look of such beatific enthrallment that a stunned Jase lost all track of his delphine connections. All he could see was the woman before him. He could feel her exhilarated movements in his arms, hear her delighted cries, and he wished the perfect moment would never end…

But even in The Sanctuary, perfection was a rare and fleeting thing.

A huge school of common feeder fish passed outside the lagoon in the deeper waters. Jase heard the message pass with rapid speed from one dolphin to another, felt the attention shift from the newcomer and himself to the potential prey.

Yes, go feed, my friends. The dolphins heard the reluctance in his voice—reluctance to see that look of delight fade from Geneva's face—and they hesitated. Jase was forced to strengthen his message. *Go, go, go. Food is waiting. Hurry, now. Yes, it's all right. You may leave. Hurry. Hurry!*

Just as rapidly as it had filled, the lagoon emptied, until only a single pair of recently fed bottle-nose lingered. With a sigh, Jase focused once more on the woman in his arms.

"Oh, Jase," Geneva whispered.

It was all she said. There were no rapturous comments, no delirious outpourings, no words trying to analyze what she'd just seen. But in that simple "Oh, Jase," he heard everything he'd hoped to hear. And felt in his gut a deep triumph, a primitive male punch of excitement that he'd pleased her.

"You liked it," he stated, his arms still around her waist, where he had placed them to steady her.

She nodded. "Thank you. It was…beautiful." She shook her head in wonderment, then dropped her hands to gently stroke the silky body of one floating bottle-nose. "And so are you," she whispered, her gaze averted.

"Me?" he said hesitantly. "Me, Geneva?" The man in him was taken totally unawares. Even the skilled psychologist in him honestly didn't know what to say—what to think, what to do.

So he kissed her.

When she didn't resist, he kissed her again.

And again.

And again.

Her lips tasted of salt from the sea. But the taste of her mouth wasn't bitter seawater. It was the sweet freshness of nectar, the taste of a woman full of life, full of emotion. And he wanted it—*wanted her*—even though she was from a world he'd left so long ago.

He felt Geneva's response to his touch, felt the tightening of her arms around his neck, felt the arching of her body as he opened her mouth to his, allowing him to taste more deeply.

In his mind he felt the two bottle-nose pick up on his excitement and send their approval.

Yes, you're right. You were right all along. This woman is my mate. I want her. I need her... His every nerve fired with a ferocious primal urge to have Geneva all to himself—an urge the dolphins recognized. *Leave me!* he ordered them. They obeyed.

A distracted Geneva lifted her head from his lips as the bottle-noses launched into the air only mere inches from them and immediately headed out toward open sea. But her eyes only tracked the dolphins for a few seconds before her attention, and her hands and her mouth, were back on Jase.

"Remember what you told me, Geneva," he said hoarsely. "You wouldn't start anything you didn't want to finish."

"I remember," she whispered. Just like she remembered her vow to stay uninvolved until she saw Thomas again. Cold logic warred with the yearning both her body and her soul cried out for—and logic lost. Reason meant nothing in Jase's presence. Reason belonged only in the real world. It didn't belong in The Sanctuary. The Sanctuary was magic....

She smiled a totally feminine Mona Lisa smile, and slowly peeled the straps of her suit down off her arms. She stopped when she reached the waterline at her waist, her fingers still grasping the straps.

Jase shivered with desire as she exposed her breasts. They were a beautiful shade of ivory, gently tipped with beige, and framed with strands of ebony hair. His hands tightened on her waistline while his eyes feasted on the sight.

"Your breasts are beautiful," he said hoarsely. "More beautiful than I'd imagined." Jase made no move to touch them. For now, just looking at the beige and ivory, just tracing the tiny blue lines of her veins with his eyes as they tracked over the gentle swells was enough. And the anticipation of touching them was a pleasure-pain he felt building, all the pent-up passion of years of loneliness rushing forth.

Still he hesitated. "Geneva, are you sure?" he asked hoarsely. "We both know there can be no future for us."

Her answer was to lift her hands from her suit and place them around his neck. He watched as her breasts lifted proudly at the action, then brushed against his chest, causing his blood to surge at the motion. He could feel her own want in the sudden pliancy of her body, feel how ready, how receptive, she was for his touch.

And it was then that looking wasn't enough. Ever so gently he reached for the side of her right breast with one forefinger. The sensation was exquisite. Suddenly the silky skins of his dolphins seemed harsh, almost rough in comparison.

Geneva leaned into his touch. With his finger, he followed one of the tiny blue lines up to the areola. And delicately traced the perfect circle of beige.

He'd forgotten how responsive a woman's breast could be. Before his eyes, the circle darkened, swelled and blossomed. He lifted his single finger, then lowered it over her distended nipple. He felt the hot heat beneath him and knew he wouldn't back off now.

Couldn't.

He savored the firm, textured beauty of her, even as he savored the pleasure on her face. Ever so slowly he covered her breast with his hand, pressing against her until her pliant curve molded itself, imprinting its exquisite shape against his palm.

He guided her into shallower, ankle-deep water. He released her to reach for the maillot, but Geneva's hands were there before his. She bent at the waist and began to pull it down. Jase's breath caught in his throat as her breasts swayed slightly at the motion, their ivory color contrasting with the light tan on her arms.

He fleetingly wondered how she'd look if she was tan all over, like him. Wondered if he would be able to see those delicate blue veins if she was. Wondered if he'd like her better all ivory or all tan and was unable to decide. Each shade of her skin seemed perfect for her. He agonized over the choice in his mind, picturing her first one way then the other.

Then she was gloriously naked, and all his thoughts stopped.

Geneva awkwardly held the wet suit in one hand, uncertain what to do with it. At Jase's wanton, hungry gaze she suddenly blushed and covered herself, one hand across her breasts, the suit covering the area below her waist.

God, she was beautiful. The artist in him recognized the pose of shyness and sensuality.

"You look like Botticelli's Venus," he whispered, his voice hoarse with awe, the blood pounding through his body with hot, fierce desire.

Geneva heard his words, which affected her more than any man's ever had. But then, Jase affected her more than any man ever had. His compliment gave her the courage to drop the arm across her breasts, and drop the suit. It fell into the water at her ankles with a soft *plop*.

Jase neither saw it fall, nor heard its splash. His senses were filled with only her. His eyes greedily drank in the graceful lines of her neck framed in glistening black hair. They traveled over her breasts and past her lush hips to stop at the neat triangle far below her navel.

He wasn't conscious of doing it, but he must have reached for her, pulled her to him, because Geneva was suddenly in his arms. As she pulled off his swimsuit, he pulled her down to the warm Sanctuary sands.

"You want me," she whispered. "And I want you. Make love to me, Jase Guardian."

Had his wildest fantasies suddenly come true? Jase felt the heat and pressure in his loins surge even fiercer, more intense. He hadn't thought it possible for him to become more aroused than he already was, but Geneva Kelsey was now doing just that—pushing him dangerously close to the edge with her simple, soft words.

Long-forgotten sensations and deliberately buried emotions flared into life. The feel of her soft, lithe body on top of his was more than he'd ever dreamed of.

The loneliness deep inside his soul cried for relief. The rustle of her wet hair against his skin whispered of things to come. The feel of her breasts against his bare chest, the perfect cradle of her thighs resting exquisitely, heavily, against him awakened an urge for love he thought long buried.

How could he have forgotten that it felt like this? Or had it ever felt like this?

The lagoon lapped at his shoulders as he pulled her toward his mouth, the dragging friction of her upward movement sending shudders down his spine and blood rushing to all three erectile areas of his body. Jase arched involuntarily in the water, then rolled over, his lips still hard on hers. Geneva was now beneath him, her eyes closed, her mouth locked with his.

The water lifted her hair and floated it over one cheek.

He refused to break the kiss as he scooped his hand beneath her neck and lifted her, keeping her face free of the water while moving her head back on exposed sand. The rest of her lay perpendicular to the waterline, cushioned by a turquoise ocean and blanketed by bronze male skin.

"Now, Jase, *now!*" she said, shifting beneath him with an urgent request he couldn't help but recognize—and satisfy.

With exquisite care he slowly guided himself into her. Geneva sighed with pleasure and slowly shifted once more beneath him.

"Don't move, Geneva. *Please* don't move just yet," he said in a strangled voice.

"I want to move," she whispered, her hands encircling his neck. "I want to make *you* move." And she lifted her hips against him again, her hands coming between them to slowly slide up and down his chest, her palms caressing, urging, pleading.

"Don't…you…want…to…" Despite himself, his hips pressed once, twice, into hers. "Take your time?" The last three words came out in a rush.

"No." She moved against him again, and Jase felt his chest, his muscles and his groin tighten, then keep tightening with excruciating need. Still he managed to resist. He wanted to pleasure her first. But Geneva Kelsey was driving away his last shreds of control.

For the first time Jase realized that his wild, passionate abandon had nothing to do with five years of celibacy. It had *everything* to do with Geneva. He suspected that his body and heart would always react this way with this particular woman, that he'd never get enough of her.

But he'd be damned if he'd leave her unsatisfied. He started to pull away from her, to break the union he wanted so very badly. He would take his pleasure later. For now, Geneva came first.

Something in his face must have given him away, for Geneva locked her legs around his hips in response and drew him closer. Before Jase could protest, her hands cupped his neck to press him even harder down against her.

As her body moved again and again with agonizing pleasure, the feeling in his groin demanded satisfaction, yet still Jase resisted. Years without touching a woman, without even hearing a woman's voice, meant nothing. The raging torment between his thighs meant nothing. The wish to revel in primitive splendor—deep inside her—meant nothing.

If it couldn't be both of them, it would be neither of them, Jase vowed. The sharing was the best part of his own physical fulfillment, and his partner's pleasure was *all* of his emotional pleasure. He couldn't just take. So with every ounce of formidable control Jase had, he resisted, even as she continued to move.

Until he heard her soft gasping cry, felt her hands clutch frantically at his shoulders and saw her neck tip back farther and farther until her chin pointed at the tropical sun. Until—in stunned wonder—Jase felt Geneva's body shudder around his in release.

And he could resist no longer.

His own release was hard, reckless, almost violent. But even in the throes of an overwhelming climax, his thoughts were on Geneva. Even as his body fired with wave after wave of pleasure, he was aware of her hands reaching for him and holding him, holding him even after his shudders subsided and the soft sand and shallow waters supported them both.

Jase collapsed against her, an equal combination of stunned surprise and heavenly gratification flooding through his limp body. He drew in a gasping breath, rolled onto his back so she was no longer pinned beneath him, but was above him, still in his arms, and closed his eyes.

Beautiful. Just beautiful... He couldn't speak. He could only lay there, his body relaxed in the blissful contentment that was almost as pleasurable as the release itself—the blissful contentment that was Geneva in his arms. He only hoped that she'd felt what he had.

Not just pleasure, but something more.

It was Geneva who lifted her head from his shoulder and spoke first. "Jase..." she said in wonder.

He saw that she was at a loss for words herself and felt a thrill of pure male pride. He smiled and tenderly stroked her cheek.

Geneva reached up to cover his hand with her own. "You're going to have to rename this place," she said breathlessly. "I don't think 'The Sanctuary' quite gives the right impression."

Jase smoothed the hair he'd tangled during their lovemaking. "And what would you suggest?" he asked, amused at her words. "Fantasy Island?"

"That's not a bad title," Geneva said with a smile, "but it's been done before. I was thinking more along the lines of Paradise Island."

"Paradise?" Jase tried to hide his look of satisfaction, and failed miserably. "Are you saying everything was *perfect?*"

Geneva nestled her head on his shoulder. "Well, almost perfect. If I could only see Thomas..."

Jase recoiled violently from her words.

Damn her! She hadn't trusted him, after all!

Chapter Seven

The hot passion in his blood was replaced by icy daggers of fury as he realized exactly what Geneva Kelsey had just done. She'd tried to buy her way to her brother with her body. Nothing more, nothing less.

The hands that so tenderly held her body clenched into fists. He wanted to scream, to rant, to rave, at the injustice of it all.

Jase Guardian did none of these things. Drawing on over five years of control, Jase merely retreated, both physically and emotionally. He stared at her with cold eyes and told himself he didn't care.

He swore to himself he didn't care.

"Jase?"

He refused to answer that soft entreaty.

"Jase, what's wrong?"

He pushed her away from him and tossed her the swimsuit and wraparound skirt. "Get dressed," he ordered, the vicious sting of his voice making her wince.

Geneva stared at him with wide eyes that opened even wider as realization struck. "Oh, Jase, it's not what you think!" she cried. "Thomas had nothing to do with this! You've misunderstood!"

Jase deliberately turned his back on her. He heard

the quiet sounds of her dressing, then got dressed and told himself it was for the best. The piercing pain inside his soul was proof enough of that.

When the quiet sounds of dressing stopped, he turned around again. "Go back to the house. Don't leave until I get back."

Geneva grabbed at his arm, her eyes dark with emotion. "I'm not going anywhere until I set things straight between us."

Jase walked away from her toward the water.

"Jase, please!" she begged. "Where are you going?"

Jase refused to speak to her. His face felt stiff, but the rest of him felt bruised and battered. And totally, utterly alone. *Again.*

"When will you be back?"

That question he was willing to answer. He turned and faced her one last time. "When I can look at your lovely face without wanting to break your neck."

Geneva gasped, but she stood her ground. "Jase…"

"Go to the house, Geneva. *Now.*"

After a moment's hesitation, she did.

Jase watched her leave. In the blink of an eye, the splendor of the day had been cruelly torn away. And the strength of that impact had threatened to strip away what small amount of peace he'd managed to regain since the deaths of Nanci and his dolphins in the clinic.

Jase reeled from the blow and desperately fought to regain some semblance of stability. God knows how long it would take him to recover. But one thing was clear. Geneva Kelsey didn't belong in The Sanctuary. The sooner he got her out of here the better. Jase knew where she belonged, just as he knew where *he* belonged. The Sanctuary and his wards were his only salvation.

Jase stepped toward the water, then stopped at the reflection of the spandex suit in the clear shallows. With sudden revulsion he ripped it off his body, hurled it high up onto the beach and dived nude into the water. He didn't need the trappings of civilization any more than he needed a hole in the head.

Or a knife in the heart...

GENEVA WATCHED JASE SWIM far out into the lagoon, then dive under the breakers that signaled the end of the reef and the start of deeper waters. From there he was lost to sight.

The deep joy she'd felt at being one with Jase had turned to deep despair. She'd finally acknowledged the feelings that had bloomed and grown steadily since the first time she'd met him. Despite her concern for Thomas and her continued ignorance of his whereabouts, she'd generously offered her heart to Jase Guardian.

And he'd misunderstood her completely! He actually thought she was offering him her body to try to buy a meeting with Thomas!

Geneva cringed at the thought. Jase was so wrong! Didn't he know that, rightly or wrongly, Thomas always seemed to take a back seat when she and Jase were together?

So now she had *two* problems. Convincing a mystery man she cared while at the same time finding Thomas. She didn't know which task would prove to be harder.

Some time after waking from her drugged sleep Geneva had felt for her twin with her mind. There had been nothing, no response, no empathy, only a vast emptiness that had been with her since the plane's disappearance. What she had prayed for—that their "twin thing" would work once she crossed the barriers—hadn't happened. Was Thomas out of practice because he'd given up on finding her again? Or, worse yet, had Jase lied to her, after all?

No, that couldn't be true. Geneva refused to accept it. Every instinct she possessed swore that Jase was telling the truth. Just as she'd told him the truth with her heart, her body and her soul. Until she'd made a stupid comment about Thomas that Jase had totally misinterpreted.

Jase, where are you?

For a few more moments she continued to stare out the window. Finally she turned away—and found herself staring straight at the seated figure of an elderly man.

"Don't be frightened," he said. "I'm a friend of Jase's."

Geneva hadn't heard the elderly man come in, yet despite being startled, she instinctively knew he meant well. Her muscles relaxed as she dropped the defensive pose she'd adopted.

"I'm sorry, sir," she said respectfully. "But he's not here."

The man sighed, but his eyes were kind. "Why does everyone insist on calling me that?"

"I—" Geneva thought about that as she took a caned bamboo seat across from the one in which the man was seated. "You look like a *sir*," she replied.

And it was true. There was an air of authority about him, a calm assurance, that she couldn't help but notice. True, Jase also had those qualities, but Jase didn't possess the aura of ageless wisdom that this man had. Geneva was certain this man held a high, if not the highest, position here in The Sanctuary.

"And you, Miss Geneva Kelsey, look very unhappy."

"You know my name!"

"Of course. There are not that many newcomers to The Sanctuary, and the marine creatures here talk much. As do my guardians." He smiled and adjusted his flowing robes. In any other man the action would have seemed effeminate, but to Geneva, the move seemed almost regal.

A sudden thought crossed her mind.

"What caused that almost-smile, Geneva?"

Geneva felt foolish, but somehow she couldn't shrug off the older man's query. "For a moment you reminded me of a picture I saw of Poseidon. But I can hardly go around calling you that, now, can I?"

"I usually go by the title of Senior Guardian." The older man's eyes twinkled, and Geneva was glad he wasn't upset at her nonsense.

"I'll remember, sir," Geneva said, not asking for his real name when he didn't volunteer it. She was content to call him sir, knowing it was appropriate. "And I meant no disrespect. I'm usually very levelheaded. It's just…that I've had a very strange day. It started out so good, but…" She rubbed at her temples with shaking fingers.

The older man leaned forward in his chair, inviting her confidence. "I am a good listener, my child."

Geneva hesitated. She certainly wasn't going to bare her soul to some stranger, especially when it came to her feelings for Jase and what they'd just experienced. Despite being emotionally upset, her body was still pleasurably satiated from Jase's lovemaking. She'd never felt anything like the two of them together, ever, and she was no blushing schoolgirl. What's more, she wanted to feel his body covering hers again. And *again*. Those were hardly the thoughts to share with anyone, let alone the man she suspected was Jase's boss.

"Let's just say Jase and I had a slight misunderstanding," she said vaguely. "I'm waiting for him to get back to straighten things out."

The Senior Guardian nodded. "I am glad to hear that. Jase has a very high opinion of you."

"Really?" Geneva said eagerly. Then her smile died. "But how could you know?"

He smiled. "His wards talk to my wards. They all speak of Jase's respect and admiration for his mate."

Geneva's cheeks flushed ever so slightly at the word *mate*, but she refused to confirm or deny anything. "I'm afraid that's a moot point either way. Jase has his world, and I have mine. The two never cross except for business, right?" she said with sad eyes. "And I'm afraid that's all Jase thinks I'm interested in. Business." *In the form of Thomas.*

"And nothing could be further from the truth?"

"No. I didn't mean to cause him pain. He misunderstood." Geneva sighed. "Jase is so hard to figure out. And I suppose it's just as hard for him to understand me."

The older man gave her a compassionate smile. "Perhaps, once his own pain and confusion diminish, Jase will understand. And forgive."

"Do you think so?" Geneva didn't add how important that was to her, nor did she know that the desperation in her eyes spoke volumes.

"Yes. Jase has a big heart where others are concerned." Geneva's sigh of relief was cut short as the man added, "Unfortunately, he is not as generous when it comes to forgiving himself."

"Can you tell me why he's so alone?"

"That is for him to do, my child, not me. I only ask that you be patient with Jase. He is a very lonely man."

Geneva clasped her hands tightly in her lap. "He told me he hadn't been with a woman in five years."

The Senior Guardian looked off into the distance. Geneva followed his gaze and saw that Jase was swimming back in.

"Jase has not kept company with a man, woman or child in the past five years," he corrected her. "Aside from myself, you are the first human soul he has had on this island since his arrival here. My favorite guardian has been to hell, Geneva Kelsey. I would like to see him come back some day. No matter how difficult Jase is, please be kind to him."

He gave her a look of encouragement, then readjusted his robe. "Things are not always what they seem, Geneva. Those you would trust can deceive, while those you mistrust can be loyal to the death. Remember that."

Geneva looked up in surprise as he moved away from her. "Are you saying I should trust Jase?"

The older man didn't answer right away. "Did you know Geneva means White Wave? A lovely name. It was always a favorite of mine. As for Jase..." He shook his head.

Geneva looked out the window and saw Jase emerge from the water. "What about Jase?" she asked, her eyes on the younger man, not the older. She watched him pull the swimsuit up over his thighs to cover his naked buttocks and felt another wanton flush of desire surge through her. They'd made love only a short time ago, and yet she was ready, yes, even eager for Jase again.

There was no answer to her question. "Sir?" Geneva whirled around. Her eyes frantically searched the room. "Sir?"

The Senior Guardian was gone.

Geneva sat back down on the bamboo chair, her skirt tangled around her knees, her thoughts a tangled web in her head. She watched as Jase made his way up the path. Something about his bowed head affected her more than she cared to admit. Then and there, she resolved to repair some of the damage she'd done, even if she had to refrain from the subject of Thomas. She hadn't seen her brother for the past two decades. A little more time couldn't possibly make a difference.

If, that is, Thomas was still alive....

If the Senior Guardian was right...

If Jase could be trusted...

JASE TRUDGED SLOWLY up the beach. His white-hot fury of earlier was gone. He tried to resign himself to the problems that obtaining the Steller's sea cows had created: the biggest problem, of course, being Geneva Kelsey. Funny how her presence had pushed the sirenian pair to the background. Funnier still how right it felt to have Geneva as his top priority.

No, funny was the wrong word for it. He cared passionately, deeply, wholeheartedly, for Geneva Kelsey. Suddenly he was sick and tired of being alone. Tired of living with only the past and old nightmares for a sleeping companion. He wanted Geneva for a sleeping companion, a waking companion, a lifetime companion...a mate.

Geneva made him forget old wounds, old scars. More important, she'd made him feel alive again, willing to give and accept love. She'd made him think of the future, a future with the two of them together. The prize Jase desperately sought had abruptly changed. It wasn't just the Steller's sea cows he coveted. It was Geneva Kelsey herself.

Jase stopped to check on the nesting progress of a pair of whooping cranes, his hands carefully parting the grasses so as not to disturb them, his mind awhirl with possibilities. The Sanctuary needed guardians. There were always more positions to go around than could be filled, for The Sanctuary was very choosy when it came to bestowing its gifts.

Geneva had the knowledge and the personality to receive those gifts, of that Jase was certain. Even without any special powers, she was still a damn fine marine biologist. She'd be a perfect asset to The Sanctuary. And a perfect partner for one Jason Merrick. He was willing to fight for her. All he had to do was convince her to stay.

Jase resumed his trek back to the house, reviewing the situation. There was no getting around their business deal. Thomas Kelsey would be set free in exchange for the sea cows. But once that was taken care of, maybe Geneva would be so grateful to see how well The Sanctuary had taken care of her brother that she would be more receptive to his advances.

And Jase certainly planned on making more of them.

First he'd tempt her with all his rare, exotic species. And then he'd dazzle her with himself. Once upon a

time he'd been charming, witty and attractive to the
ladies. No woman had ever complained about his personality, his looks or his performance in bed. And with
Geneva as his partner, his lovemaking had been elevated to an art form: a veritable masterpiece that was
Geneva and him together.

The memory of Geneva's unclothed body flashed
through his mind. The memory of her moving sensuously beneath him, above him, around him, was doing
strange things to his insides. The sooner he had her in
his arms again the sooner he could show her how
much he wanted her to stay.

Oh, yes. It was time—*way* past time—to resurrect
his old self. The prize was more than worth it.

A look of resolve crossed Jase's face. Maybe the
Senior Guardian was right. Maybe it was time to stop
acting like some morose, Byronic hero and act like a
red-blooded American male again. He'd had five long
years of being the strong silent type. Now he wanted
to smile, to laugh, to love again.

Geneva Kelsey was the perfect solution. He would
convince her to become a guardian here in The Sanctuary. It shouldn't be hard. After returning with the
Steller's sea cows, she'd stay of her own free will—
with a little help from him.

And what if she doesn't want to stay? a tiny little
voice nagged him. Jase pushed it away, refusing to
worry. *If she doesn't,* he told himself, *I'll just have to
find another way to convince her.*

IT WASN'T UNTIL JASE was more than halfway up the
beach that Geneva noticed a change in him. She
couldn't exactly pinpoint when the difference occurred, but his step had a spring in it again, and he

carried himself proudly. Geneva desperately hoped it meant Jase was in a better frame of mind. She withdrew from the window when he was closer and hurried down the path to meet him.

To her relief, he gave her a friendly nod. "Hello, Geneva."

She sent him a tentative smile. "I was hoping you'd come back."

"Of course I'd come back. Where else would I go, Geneva?" He gave her an amused smile. "It's almost noon, and you slept through breakfast. I'm here to fix you something to eat."

"I—" Geneva couldn't get over the change in him. "After everything that's just happened, you want to talk about food?" she asked incredulously.

"I never starve my guests. What would you like to eat?"

"Whatever you're having, but, Jase, we need to talk!" she insisted.

"Later." Jase tucked her arm into his. He didn't release her until they were inside the bungalow and the kitchen area.

Geneva couldn't stand the suspense any longer. "Jase, forget about the meal for a minute. I'm sorry about earlier," she added in a rush.

"Sorry about our lovemaking?" He gave her a telling look. "I'm certainly not, Geneva. In fact, I was hoping we could do it again," he said bluntly.

Geneva blinked with surprise, then tried to ignore her traitorous body's weakening as he bent over and began rummaging among the pots and pans. She had to make him understand. "Jase, I'm not referring to…that."

Jase straightened, holding a frying pan. Only this

time there was a smile on his face. "Thank goodness. I'd hate to think I was the only one who felt the earth move."

Geneva felt her cheeks warm as her body temperature rose several degrees. "Would you please be quiet and listen to me?" she begged. "I want to explain about what I said about Thomas. I don't want you to think that I'd ever—"

"Use your body to bribe me so you could see Thomas?" Jase interrupted. "I know that, Geneva. I just needed a little time to think things through."

Geneva felt a rush of gratitude—and love—surge at his words. He'd made it so easy for her, and she thought it would be so difficult. "I'm glad, Jase. I was so worried that you'd misinterpreted. What happened between us meant so much to me, and I was afraid I'd ruined it.…" Her voice trailed off in embarrassment.

Jase immediately abandoned the frying pan and placed his arms around her. "No, I'm the one who ruined it," he softly admitted, his fingers lacing themselves through her hair. "In fact, I probably owe you an apology." He lowered his lips to hers and proceeded to give her a most thorough "apology."

When Geneva finally came up for air, she marveled at the change in him. And in herself. She'd gone from joy to agony and back to bliss again. Jase had more power over her than she'd thought. And suddenly that didn't seem like such a bad thing.

"You know, the Senior Guardian did tell me you wouldn't be angry with me for long, but I wasn't sure," she said.

Jase gave her one last caress, then turned back toward the stove. "The Senior Guardian was here?"

"Yes. He kept me company while you were gone."

"That's a surprise. He rarely makes social calls. It appears you're a very popular lady, Geneva Kelsey." Jase reached for an onion and a paring knife. "And just what did he say to you?" he asked casually.

"Not much." She took a seat on the high stool next to the work island. "He said you wouldn't be angry and that you were a good guardian."

"That's all?" Jase asked.

"Yes. Well, no," she corrected herself. "He said he liked my name."

"Geneva is a beautiful name. Is that all he said?"

Geneva watched as Jase brought out the fresh fish, coconut milk and mangoes that would be their meal.

"He said..." Geneva took a deep breath. "He wanted to know if I was your mate."

"Ah." Jase put the fish and onions in the pan to fry. "And just what did you tell him?"

"I never kiss and tell," she said with a smile. But then her smile faded. "Even if I did, Jase, I wouldn't know what to tell him. I don't even know the answer to that myself." She met his gaze head on. "You know I can't stay here with you, Jase."

"And I can't leave when you go," he said quietly.

Geneva looked at him with sad eyes and was silent.

"Let's just enjoy what we have and leave it at that for now, okay?" Jase said.

Geneva nodded, wishing things could be different. *If only there could be more...*

An hour later they had eaten, cleared up and finished the dishes.

"Perhaps you'd like to lie down?" he suggested. "You've been through a lot lately. With all the time you spent in the water, you're probably tired, too."

"Oh, but I'm not! What I'd really like to do is—"

She saw Jase tense again and was certain he expected her to bring up Thomas again.

"Go outside. I noticed some parrots—all endangered species. And if I haven't totally lost my mind, you have some dodo and moa birds on your island. I'd like to see them up close."

Her words put a broad smile on his face. Jase threw the dish towel across the dish rack to dry and reached for her arm.

"You've got yourself a deal."

A few hours later Geneva was exhausted. She'd happily traipsed every inch of land on Jase's island but was still eager for more.

"I've counted fifteen supposedly extinct birds and reptiles!" She and Jase were watching *Rhodonessa caryophyllacea* feed in a small freshwater pond. "I can't believe my eyes. This pink-headed duck is supposed to be extinct like all the others!"

"They nest only on my island," Jase said proudly. He reached for her hand and walked her slowly over to where the duck's eggs were laid. "Some of the bigger islands have aurochs, quagga and great auks," he said, the three which were an extinct—at least, according to Geneva's textbooks—horned bovine, a zebralike equine and a bird. "But my fresh water is limited, so I'm only allowed to keep the smaller animals. The moas are about as big as it gets here."

Geneva watched as he pointed. Sure enough, a brown-feathered moa, relative of the flightless emu and ostrich, emerged from the tropical growth to drink from the pond.

"What? No passenger pigeons?" Geneva whispered so as not to disturb the large creature.

"That's another island," Jase said matter-of-factly.

Geneva glanced at him sharply but saw that he wasn't joking.

"I wish I'd brought a camera," she moaned with frustration.

"I would have had to destroy all your film," Jase said.

"But then no one would believe that— Oh." *Of course.* "It makes sense, I suppose." But she couldn't help being disappointed.

"Sorry, Geneva. No pictures of my wards are allowed. We can't afford to let anyone know we're here."

The moa wandered off, and Jase waded with Geneva to a rock perched on the edge of a small, trickling waterfall. They both sat and dangled their bare feet in the water. The pink-headed duck quacked noisily for a few seconds, then calmed down and settled on her eggs.

"How do you keep people from discovering The Sanctuary?" Geneva asked curiously. "I'm certain these islands have been here for centuries, yet none of them are on any marine charts."

"The violent weather patterns here in the Caribbean help for starters. The barriers are so imposing that most potential trespassers turn tail. And of course we have a group of PR people who do their very best to spread all kinds of crazy rumors about the Devil's Triangle."

"*Your* people are the ones responsible for those hokey stories about Atlantis and sea monsters and UFOs?"

"Sure," Jase said with a grin. "Sailors are a very superstitious lot. Why sail through the triangle when it's just as easy to go around it? The same goes for the air traffic. We get a minimum of trespassers, and our islands are left intact.''

''Talk about your sensational journalism,'' Geneva remarked.

Immediately Jase's arm lifted and curled around her shoulder. ''I know it must be hard for the grieving family who has to listen to such nonsense. It couldn't have been easy for you.''

''No, it's okay, Jase,'' Geneva said, touched by his compassion. ''That's a small price to pay for keeping people away, and for ensuring the survival of rare species.''

''I'm glad you understand.'' His fingers lightly stroked her bare skin. ''The sad thing is, while we have the water mass for preserving just about all of the saltwater species, we can't do the same for the freshwater species, or the creatures on land.''

''Can't a land sanctuary be started?''

''No. For one thing, it couldn't be kept a secret like this place. Fortunately, the nation's zoo system handles the endangered land species quite well. They're doing a good job preserving animals that are extinct in the wild.''

''Like the Mongolian wild horse and the Arabian oryx,'' Geneva murmured.

''Exactly. But as for marine sanctuaries, we're it.'' Still holding on to her shoulder, Jase fished a dead twig out of the water and swished away a pesky dragonfly from her legs.

''I was hoping to start a sirenian institute in Alaska,'' Geneva said with a sigh.

''I know it's not going to help your career to lose the sea cows, Geneva. But we have no choice but to bring your sea cows here. Your own native Inuit still club seals to death, along with other hunters whose motives are less honorable than your people's. Whales are still caught and slaughtered outside of Alaska by the Russians, and bears continue to be shot, stuffed and mounted outside of trading posts.''

"Alaska's come a long way in its conservation efforts,'' Geneva said defensively. "We've made a lot of progress.''

"True. Until the next cruise ship dumps its garbage off Alaska's shores, or the next supertanker spills its cargo of oil all over Alaska's waters. And where will your Steller's sea cows be then?''

Geneva drew in a shaky breath. "Granted, this country has a long way to go yet in its conservation efforts. But we *are* working at it!'' she insisted. "What you and the other guardians do here in The Sanctuary is all very well and good, Jase, but it isn't a solution! Education is the key to conservation efforts. People need to be taught to protect our natural habitats. Hiding all these beautiful animals away is like—''

Geneva searched wildly for a good example, her hands palms up in the air. "It's like locking up the *Mona Lisa* or *The Last Supper* from the public because they haven't been trained to appreciate art!''

"As I recall, Michelangelo's *Pietà* was disfigured by some madman with a hammer,'' Jase easily countered. "The same types of people rake their boat propellers across marine mammals' backs.''

"You can't give up on the whole because of a few lunatics!'' Geneva insisted. "It's easy for *you* to hide your specimens on some mysterious land. I can't!''

"Can't you? Have you ever seriously considered doing just that, Geneva?''

Geneva froze at the thought. "Stay here?"

"Exactly."

"But...what about my work?"

"You'd have your work here in The Sanctuary. You'd have the sea cows, and I'd make you their guardian. After a while, you'd be able to talk to them just like I talk to my dolphins."

"Me? Become a guardian?" *And stay here with you?* The thought was so tempting that Geneva felt its draw like a physical urge.

"Why not? Your marine parks are fighting a losing battle. So are your marine biologists. Why not come here where you can do some real good?"

Geneva forced herself to remain logical. "I *am* doing some real good, Jase. The Steller's sea cows would never have been found, would never have a chance to make a comeback without my efforts. The Sanctuary didn't find them! No guardian who talks to animals found them! A plain old ordinary biologist did. Not someone like you. Someone like *me!*"

"That's true. But think how much more you could do if you were someone like *me*." Jase's eyes were unfathomable, and his expression just as hard for Geneva to read as he spoke. "It is possible, Geneva. All you have to do is pledge your loyalty to The Sanctuary. Just say yes, and all this can be yours."

Geneva felt herself actually weakening. Could she give up family, friends and her life's work to stay in The Sanctuary? To stay with Jase? To have him at her side, day and night, and not have to share him with another person ever?

"And don't forget, along with the sea cows, Thomas would be here for you, too. We don't have to send him home if you don't want."

Geneva moaned and flung herself off the rock. She had to get away from that magnetic pull that was Jase Guardian. Quickly she waded through the water, setting the pink-headed duck to flight. It landed a distance away and nervously watched its nest. Geneva saw it ruffle its feathers, afraid to come close. She knew how it felt. In her present frame of mind, she was afraid to be near Jase Guardian. Afraid she wanted to stay with him in his world, and leave hers behind.

And that would mean leaving it behind forever....

Geneva stood in the water, trembling. After a moment, Jase came after her.

"I think we're disturbing the duck," Jase said as Geneva struggled to pull herself together. "Maybe we should leave her in peace." He took her hand and they waded back to the shore.

"I'm tired," Geneva said, suddenly feeling the strain of the past twenty-four hours. Her legs ached, her back ached and her stomach felt iffy at best. "Which way back to the bungalow?"

"This way," he said. Jase offered her his arm, but Geneva was afraid to take it, afraid to let him work his spell over her again. She couldn't let him influence her. She couldn't make him any promises until she saw that Thomas was safe and sound. She let Jase take the lead and deliberately walked behind him, where his potent brand of magic couldn't touch her.

Even though she desperately wished it would...

Geneva couldn't help but remember his touch and their lovemaking. She stumbled over a tangled root system, then swore out loud. Jase stopped and hurried to her side.

"I'm okay," she insisted as she regained her balance, suddenly feeling an overpowering wave of homesickness. At least back in Florida everything made sense, which was more than she could say about this mystical, magical place.

She should be home with her co-workers, and Marnee—good old Marnee the manatee—and watching good old Oprah over her TV dinner. Geneva bit her trembling lip as Jase hovered protectively. What would Oprah say if she could see her now?

Kidnapped sirenian expert escapes from Bermuda Triangle! Next! On Oprah!

Only what would Oprah recommend to a woman with the last two Steller's sea cows on earth and a missing twin brother whose fate depended on those same cows? What would she advise for a woman falling in love with her brother's captor?

Geneva sank to the soft tropical soil cross-legged and buried her face in her hands.

Jase lowered himself beside her. "Are you all right?"

"I don't feel very good," Geneva moaned.

"Stomach upset? Headache?"

"Yes."

"Shaky arms and legs?"

Geneva nodded.

"Feeling like crying?"

"No!" Only she did. Why else would the thought of missing her favorite TV talk-show hostess bring tears to her eyes?

"It's the antidote. It can have some lousy side effects. I once saw a very spit-and-polish Navy sailor go on a two-hour crying jag." Jase sighed. "I should have let you sleep off the sedative naturally, but that takes the better part of a day, and the dolphins wanted to meet you. Geneva, I'm sorry."

"Save your sorries. Go away." Geneva let her shoulders slide to the ground, her hair spilling around her. She saw Jase kneel down at her side.

"Come on and put your arms around my neck. I'll carry you back."

Geneva glared at him. "Don't do me any favors, Mr. Lock-Up-All-the-Paintings. I'm no helpless Pauline in peril."

"You'll never make it back to the bungalow on your own," Jase warned.

"That's all right with me. I'll sleep out here with the dodos. According to you and your opinion of real world conservationists, I should fit in just fine." Lord, but she felt awful. Thank goodness the soft jungle floor felt comfortable, the soil cool against her cheek.

"Will you fit in with the *crocodiles?* The ones I have with the sharp teeth and hearty appetites?"

"Yes! Just do your Dr. Doolittle thing and tell them to snack off you instead. They can start with your head."

"My *head?*"

"You bet. It's big enough for a ten-course meal."

"Don't be ridiculous," he said impatiently.

"Don't tell me what to do. Say hi to the crocs for me."

Jase suddenly grinned. "I do believe you're having a temper tantrum, Geneva. This is a side of the antidote I haven't seen before."

Geneva's response was to close her eyes.

Jase refused to leave. "Geneva?" Then, in a softer voice, "Are you awake?"

She opened her eyes. "*Now* what?"

"I don't want you sleeping out here with the crocodiles. You're too valuable to the sea cows—to *me*—for that.''

"Really?'' Geneva's ears perked up. Somehow she was starting to feel better.

"Yes. In fact, I think you're pretty extraordinary.''

"I can't talk to the animals,'' she reminded him, letting him slide one arm under her neck and another under her legs. She knew she should probably resist. Under normal circumstances, she was no helpless female. However, these were hardly ordinary circumstances or this an ordinary place. This was The Sanctuary, smack-dab in the middle of the Bermuda Triangle.

"No, but you sure can talk *my* ears off.''

"Thanks for the insult.'' But Geneva let her head rest against his shoulder as he lifted her up against his chest and started walking again. "If you don't mind, I've had my quota for today.''

To her surprise, Jase's eyes twinkled with amusement. "You probably have. Tell you what. If I show you my dugongs, would you call us even?''

"You have dugongs?'' Geneva gasped, naming the only totally saltwater dwelling sirenian species aside from the Steller's sea cows. Their native habitat was the Indo-Pacific oceans. She'd only seen dugongs once in Australia. To her regret, she'd never worked with them.

"I have dugongs,'' he assured her.

"Cute dugongs?''

Jase chuckled. "How very unscientific of you, Dr. Kelsey. But I do minister to quite a few. I'm sure I could find a *cute* one for you somewhere. If you ask me nicely, I'll even let you touch them.''

"When?" Geneva asked excitedly, ignoring her pounding head. "When can I see them?"

"Tomorrow morning. Is that soon enough?"

She smiled and impulsively leaned over to kiss his cheek. Jase's eyebrows lifted. He stopped in his tracks and studied her for such a long time that Geneva wondered what was wrong.

"You aren't going to change your mind?" she asked anxiously.

"No. Tomorrow morning we go see my dugongs. And tomorrow afternoon—" Jase took a deep breath. "Tomorrow afternoon we go see your brother."

Chapter Eight

Jase watched Geneva as she swam with the dugongs in his lagoon. After first calling the creatures for her, then reassuring them that she could be trusted, he was content to just look at Geneva interact with them without his assistance. Much to his delight, he sensed that she was as predisposed toward sirenians as he had been with his dolphins. He was certain he'd be able to let her communicate with them.

But he would save that for later, he vowed. Jase had his strategy down pat. For now, he would let the exotic creatures themselves woo her. And when that novelty wore off, he'd let her talk to them. He could share some of his powers...but he intended to use his gifts with Geneva wisely, carefully. He didn't want her to be receptive only to Sanctuary abilities.

He wanted her to be receptive to him....

Like she'd been yesterday on the beach. Just the memory of her and him in that most intimate of embraces was enough to set his insides quivering with desire. Last night he'd lain awake in his hammock watching Geneva sleep in hers a tantalizing arm's reach away. It was all he could do not to take her into his arms again. If he hadn't been such an idiot and made such an idiotic accusation earlier, he would have. But he didn't want to press his luck just yet. For now, it was enough that she'd accepted his apology.

She was so generous with herself. Even her simple kiss of gratitude last night when he'd told her he'd take her to Thomas had affected him deeply.

If only he had the luxury of a long, leisurely courtship! But Sanctuary business couldn't be delayed. His world demanded as brief a contact with the real world as possible. Jase himself had always preferred to live in the present. But now he had hopes for the future. Whenever Geneva rested her head against his chest, kissed him or smiled that lovely smile, he was positive he was making progress.

If only I had more time to convince her to stay, Jase thought to himself. He might have numerous Sanctuary powers, but even he couldn't stop the clock.

A peal of laughter rang out across the water and broke into his musing. Jase watched as a dugong gently butted Geneva's stomach with its light gray head, its tusks and split tail flukes distinguishing it from the Florida manatees that were Geneva's specialty.

A smile crossed Jase's face as he watched from the shallower depths. Geneva was treading water in the deeper section of the lagoon. Her face was vibrantly expressive, even from this distance. He could see her delight as the curious dugong continued to poke her belly with the sensitive, food-finding hairs of its snout.

"That tickles!" She giggled, then looked toward Jase, sharing her pleasure. "Jase, make them stop!" she called to him as another dugong poked at her. "You know laughing and swimming don't mix!"

Jase waved and swam toward her as he sent a firm

message winging to the playful dugongs. *Keep your distance!* he ordered. *Get away from my mate!*

Unconsciously he used the term with every fierce ounce of male protectiveness in him. The dugongs instantly recognized his primitive urge to defend the female in his territory. They retreated immediately.

"Jase, I didn't want you to send them far away!" Geneva watched as the dugongs withdrew to the far end of the lagoon. "A few yards would have been sufficient."

Jase himself was surprised by the force of his command. He hadn't meant to be so brusque with his wards.

"It's just as well," he said after a moment, treading water next to her. "There's a female in estrous entering the lagoon. In a few minutes the males will be fighting for her. The last thing you need is to get in the way of a mating herd."

"Oh, but Jase, I've never seen dugongs mating! Reproductive information on them is sketchy because they're so rare! Are you certain we couldn't observe?"

Jase shook his head. "I could, because I'm a guardian. But I'm afraid you couldn't. The males become quite aggressive. In fact, you should probably get out of the water."

He didn't miss her sigh of disappointment before she started toward shore with long, graceful strokes. He swam close beside her, stopping her progress when he could touch bottom easily, but she could not. He pulled her close, holding her against his chest, her feet dangling free in the water just above the sandy bottom.

"If you were a guardian," Jase said, basking in the feel of her arms winding around his neck, "you'd be able to feel them, even if you couldn't see them. You could sense what they were doing.''

Geneva turned toward the far-off dugongs, her eyes sad and yearning. ''Oh, Jase, what good is all my scientific knowledge if I can't apply it?''

Jase gave her a telling look. ''You could. You could apply it here in The Sanctuary.''

Geneva turned away from the dugongs and locked her gaze with his. ''Why do I get the feeling that you're trying to bribe me to stay, Jase Guardian?''

''Maybe because I am,'' he replied honestly. ''I've been so alone, Geneva, until you.''

''I've been lonely, too, Jase.'' Geneva gave him a slight smile. ''It was hard for me after my parents' death.''

Suddenly Jase realized just how very hard it *had* been for her. An Alaskan native torn from her own home and forced to spend the rest of her life on a strange, subtropical coast.... Without her parents, without her mother's people or culture, without her twin...

''In a way, you're the lucky one,'' she said with a sigh.

''Lucky? Me?'' Jase couldn't have been more shocked.

Geneva nodded. ''Everyone expects to be lonely on a deserted island. It's much harder being lonely in a city full of people.''

Jase dropped a kiss on her forehead. ''You're not in a city full of people now. And this is no ordinary island.''

''No, it's not, is it.'' Geneva gave him a sudden smile. And with that smile the mood instantly changed. The past was forgotten, their two totally different backgrounds were forgotten, and there was only the two of them…and the warm waters of the lagoon beneath a hot tropical sun.

"Make love to me, Jase," Geneva whispered. Her lips brushed a sea-salt kiss against his.

Jase kissed her back, feeling his soul cry out to possess her even as his body did the same. He removed her maillot with one hand, the other keeping her head and shoulders above the water.

"Jase?" Geneva said uncertainly as he let her suit sink into the lagoon. "Shouldn't we get out first?"

He smiled, even as he removed his own suit and let it join hers on the sandy bottom. "This is The Sanctuary. We do things a little differently here, remember?"

"In the…?" Geneva's eyes opened wide with realization as she stared at the crystal depths surrounding them. "Jase, I don't think I'll be any good at this."

Jase laughed softly as one of his hands left her waist and reached between her thighs. Geneva's breath caught audibly as he felt her body's warmth, but she didn't pull away.

"What I want us to do is hardly novel, Geneva." He gave in to the urge to let his fingers trace each and every outline of her most intimate places. "Mammals have been joining in the ocean for millions of years."

"I don't know," she said uneasily.

"Say yes, Geneva," he urged. "It's as natural as the tides. As natural as what you're feeling right now."

He touched her again. Geneva arched just once, then held even tighter to his neck. He could feel the trembling tension in her body as he explored even further, nestled even deeper and felt the shiver of her warm inner flesh.

Geneva spoke, her voice sweetly hoarse and low. "If I let you make love to me…"

"*If?*" he managed to say, trying to hang on to his sanity, trying not to yield to the temptation of that soft body. He didn't want this union to be as primitively passionate as before. He'd planned to take his time so they could both savor the moment.

"If I let you take me here in the water—" He felt Geneva swallow hard as his lips moved down and across her neck. "If I do, will you make certain your wards don't broadcast it?"

He lifted his head from her neck to gaze into her troubled eyes. Jase's passion was momentarily checked.

"I mean, I know The Sanctuary is different. And I honestly don't mind your wards being tuned in to you. But if they talk to other wards, and those wards talk to other guardians…" Her voice trailed off miserably. "I wouldn't like that, Jase."

Jase's submerged hand emerged from the water to stroke her hair. "Don't you worry, Geneva," he said fiercely. "We can be as free and open as we want. There will be only you and me."

"Really, Jase?" He watched as the desire that had died in her eyes returned. "No one else?"

"Neither ward nor guardian." His eyes fired with passion, even as his heart filled with tenderness. He pressed his lips against her temple and deliberately blocked out every single mental connection, leaving only his thoughts of the woman in his arms. "You have nothing to worry about, Sweet Survivor. Because I *don't* intend to share…."

At that, he felt her body become willing again, all hesitation and doubt gone from her face. She buried her head in his shoulder, but Jase wouldn't let it remain there for long. He turned her mouth to his, locked his legs around hers and took her under the water.

Above him, Geneva maintained their kiss, but her eyes immediately closed in the saltwater. Jase kept his open, savoring first the surprise and then the pleasure of her face as she allowed the water to cushion her. He kicked ever so gently with one foot, sending them slowly spinning lengthwise as they floated to the top.

After a quick breath of air for both, Jase took them under again. Only this time his hands were on her hips, not her waist. He waited until his back hit the sandy bottom, the sun streaming through the depths, before he aligned her body with his. And then, as the ocean began to lift his body to the surface, he pulled her down toward him and possessed her in the fullest sense of the word.

He saw Geneva's eyes open wide as he entered her, felt her legs lock around him to hold him closer. At the motion Jase felt a wave of tenderness that made his passion even sweeter. Her breasts molded sweetly against his chest as they surfaced again.

Still locked in a breathless union, both breathed again.

"Jase…" Geneva gasped, holding him tight. "How—I mean, what should I do now?"

Jase smiled. "Whatever you want, sweetness. Whatever you want." And without allowing her to speak again, he took them down into the water again.

Geneva's lashes fluttered closed once more. Jase, whose Sanctuary eyes had long grown immune to salt-

water sting, watched and waited with delicious anticipation. He didn't have to wait long. Geneva began to
stir against him, her movements exquisitely slow in
their watery medium. Her hair formed an ebony cloud
around them as he allowed her to set the pace. Her
need became his, her urging spurred him on, until both
of them were straining for release.

Jase lost track of the number of times they surfaced
and submerged. He surrendered himself solely to the
magic that was the two of them together in the envel-
oping folds of the sea. And just when he thought he
couldn't stand reaching for such enchantment any
longer, it came in one, long, shuddering wave that
swept them both along in its wake.

The power of that beauty washed away everything
that had come before it in Jase's life and left his heart
whole again.

How could he ever bear to let her go now?

That thought brought him back to reality. It was
Jase who kicked them both back to the surface; Jase
who had to stagger to the beach with Geneva's totally
pliant body; Jase who caught his breath first as they
collapsed in the shallower water just below the beach,
Geneva on top of him.

He slid an arm around her neck as they lay quietly
in afterglow. He felt Geneva's chest rising and falling
above his, and waited for her eyes to open. And when
they did, he didn't bother saying with words how won-
derful, how magical, their union had been. He was
positive she knew, just as he did.

So he gently teased her instead.

"You didn't forget to breathe again, did you?" he
asked tenderly. He could understand how repeated ex-

posure to Geneva Kelsey's lovemaking could make any man blissfully breathless. He certainly was.

"I could have drowned us both!" Her cheeks flushed a bright red. "You'd think *I'd* spent the last five years on a deserted island!"

Jase smiled. "Lord, Geneva, if this is what you're like under ordinary circumstances, I don't think I could have survived five years of your being celibate."

Her voice dropped even lower. "You must think I'm a crazy woman or something."

"Oh, no!" he protested. "Geneva, your face— If you could have seen your face…you were so beautiful." His voice trailed off, and he watched her blush with both pleasure and embarrassment. In his mind's eye he relived the rapture overtaking her. Deep inside he felt fierce triumph that he'd been the one sharing it with her.

But Geneva wasn't convinced, although her voice sounded more its normal self. "I can hear it now," she said ruefully. *"Women with overactive sex drives. Next! On Oprah!"*

Jase actually lifted his head from the sand at that. "My God, Geneva. Do they actually talk about such things on TV nowadays?"

Geneva finally met his gaze, her eyes apologetic. "I'm afraid so."

He whistled slowly through pursed lips. "I am going to *have* to watch this woman's show."

And then, she surprised him. She laughed.

And laughed. And laughed again, until she rolled off him and fell on her back in the sand. He lay next to her, one of her hands still clasped in his as peals and peals of joy rang in his ears. The symphonies, the operas and the concerts he'd heard in another lifetime…he couldn't ever recall hearing anything more exquisite.

Finally Geneva's laughter dwindled to a low, throaty chuckle. "You're a very unusual man, Jase Guardian."

He rose up on one elbow, loving the contrast of bright sand glittering in her dark hair. "Hey, I'm not the one who watches those strange talk shows."

She looked up and smiled at him, and suddenly the tension was back. The air crackled with his awareness of her, and hers of him. Desire flooded through him again, not with the surging passion of earlier but with a steady pace that was just as determined, just as potent. Jase bent over and kissed her, his fingertips gently tracing the delicate ridge of her collarbone.

"We'd better get back on the beach," Geneva said shakily. "I think I need steady ground under my feet."

Jase nodded. He pulled her up and into his arms, even as he called for the lagoon turtles to retrieve their suits and bring them to shore. "Thank you, Sweet Survivor."

Geneva's forehead wrinkled as he took the few short steps up onto dry beach. "Why do you keep calling me that?"

Jase pushed a strand of hair back from her face. "For twenty years we've called your brother The Survivor, because he survived the plane crash."

It suddenly struck Jase that Geneva hadn't mentioned her brother that whole day. Had her interest in him replaced concern about her brother? Or had she just decided discretion was the better part of valor? He wouldn't spoil the moment by asking, although he desperately hoped the reason was the former and not the latter.

"Since you're his twin, we gave you the same last name. Survivor."

"Only I'm not *the?* I'm *sweet?*"

"Yes." It sounded inane when he tried to explain it, but he went on, anyway. "Like all of us have the last name of Guardian. One of the best things about The Sanctuary is the anonymity it offers."

Jase reached the sand at the same time as the turtles. He set Geneva down and handed her the suit. She didn't bother to dress, and neither did he. They sat contentedly next to each other, enjoying the afterglow of their joining.

"But Jase, why don't you just call him Thomas Kelsey?"

"Because your brother would never tell us his name. He also wanted anonymity."

"Like you?"

"Yes. Like me."

Geneva bit her lip in confusion. "Maybe you had a good reason for concealing your origins, Jase, but Thomas didn't. If he was happy here, like you said, why would my brother refuse to tell you his name after all this time?"

"I think there are a couple of reasons," Jase said quietly. "First and foremost, he wanted to protect you. You two are twins. I'm certain he knew you were alive just as you knew he was. Thomas was afraid that if any word of his location slipped out, you'd come after him."

"I would have," Geneva said instantly.

"And then you'd be trapped here, too. Thomas didn't want that for you."

"I still don't see why he wouldn't pledge."

"I'm only guessing, but Thomas probably refused

because he desperately wanted to see you again. Without having any wards to take care of, he'd have no ties to The Sanctuary. If the opportunity ever presented itself to leave, he could do so with a clear conscience.''

Geneva slowly nodded. ''Thomas always did have the Inuits' strong sense of honor. To think he's been waiting to see me again all these years....'' Her voice trailed off.

Jase hated seeing the sadness in her eyes. It was such a contrast to the joy he had witnessed just a short time earlier.

''I know, Geneva. But we'll change all that. Why don't you get dressed?'' he kindly suggested.

When they were both clad again, he looped his arm around her waist and gently urged her up toward the path that led to his boat. ''Let's go find Thomas. You and he have waited long enough.''

Chapter Nine

From the deck of Jase's boat, Geneva peered anxiously at the island they were approaching. For once she was oblivious to the leaping dolphins and porpoises at the bow. The smaller island's coastline was rockier than that on Jase's island, but beyond the crashing waves Geneva could see lush tropical vegetation lining the shore.

Jase cut the engines, and the forward momentum of the boat stopped. Geneva turned toward Jase in confusion.

"I can't go any closer, Geneva. The rocks will tear the hull right out." Jase dropped anchor, then descended from the flying bridge to join her on the deck. "The dolphins and I will get you through the heavy surf and wait for you on the beach."

Geneva nodded. She quickly removed the wraparound of yet another beach set she'd changed into earlier, then shrugged off the light jacket she'd donned. She started to pass it to Jase's outstretched hand, then froze.

Thomas was waiting! She could *feel* her twin's anticipation.

The jacket fell to the deck as Thomas Kelsey

stepped onto the beach. Geneva gasped. He was far away, but she knew, *she knew* it was him.

She grabbed onto the deck railing to support herself. Her lips mouthed his name, and tears came to her eyes. "Jase, it's Thomas!" Her eyes flew to Jase, then back to the rocky beach. Dear lord, after all this time, it was really him!

Jase reached for her hand and held it tightly. "Ready, Geneva?"

Geneva took in a deep breath and nodded. Together they dove into the water.

The sea was fierce and frothing, not like the gentle lagoon on Jase's island. Geneva was tossed and buffeted about, but the dolphins' fins and Jase's hand offered steady support. She was maneuvered through the jagged rocks and cutting coral without a scratch and towed right up to the beach.

Thomas stood back a ways, silently watching as Geneva finally set foot on solid ground again.

"Take as long as you want," Jase said, but Geneva was already running up the beach toward her brother, her arms outstretched.

And then, incredibly, she was swept into his arms, swung off her feet into a bear hug and whirled around and around in circles. Geneva couldn't talk, couldn't even cry. All she could do was hold on to her twin and let the joy of the moment wash away the sorrow of twenty long years.

"Geneva, let me look at you," Thomas finally said. Geneva reluctantly allowed him to end the hug and step back. "My God, you're a sight for sore eyes!" And then his brotherly enthusiasm changed into the observation of a grown man. "Geneva—you're beautiful!"

Geneva gave him a shaky smile. "And, you, Thomas…" For the first time she got a good look at her twin. The skinny, gawky teenage boy was gone, replaced by a man. His features had aged, maturity bringing out a more Inuit facial look than Geneva had, who favored her father's Spanish ancestors. Thomas easily topped her height, although he wasn't quite as tall as Jase, she noticed. But his muscles were like Jase's, proudly proclaiming a swimmer's body, without an ounce of fat on it. To Geneva's surprise, Thomas wore modern, everyday clothes and sported a modern haircut instead of long, flowing hair like Jase. Except for the diver's knife strapped around his right thigh beneath his shorts and his bare feet, he looked like he could have come from any normal town or city.

Geneva had a hard time assimilating it all. Thomas looked well fed, well dressed, well-cared for. He was so—so *normal.* After meeting Jase, she expected a more primitive, strained look to her twin. But obviously Jase hadn't lied, after all. Thomas couldn't have looked better.

"Well? What's the verdict?" Thomas asked with a smile.

"You—you're all grown up," Geneva said in amazement. And then, as the sudden impact of two decades gone by sank in, the tears started to fall. Thomas swore, then he was holding her again, and they were both crying with joy.

"Please, Geneva, don't," Thomas begged. "Let's not waste our reunion with waterworks." He patted her awkwardly on the shoulder, then hugged her one last time. "Come on, let's go inside."

Geneva nodded and allowed her twin to show her to his house. Only it wasn't really a house, it was more like a luxury suite. Geneva was struck by the contrast between Jase's almost spartan, serviceable bungalow and Thomas's rich surroundings.

"Here you are," he said, showing her to an expensive couch atop luxurious carpeting, then sitting next to her, his arm around her shoulders. Thomas gave her a lopsided grin, and for a moment he looked like her brother of long ago. "Excuse the cliché—and not that I'm complaining—but what's a girl like you doing in a place like this?"

Geneva shone with happiness. "It's a long story, Thomas." She gave him a brilliant smile. "I can't believe I'm here. I still can't believe *you're* here!"

Thomas smiled back. "I can't believe you found me. I'd almost given up hope. But then every Christmas…"

"Every Christmas—" Geneva echoed, and suddenly they were both talking at once, yet understanding everything the other said.

The lonely holidays when their "twin thing" worked…

Thomas's survival of the plane crash…

Geneva's refusal to accept Thomas's death…

Thomas's refusal to become a guardian…

Her discovery of the Steller's sea cows…

His determination to leave The Sanctuary and go home…

Her first encounter with Jase Guardian…

And finally, incredibly, their meeting now.

"I really get to go home?" Thomas said, his voice hoarse with eagerness. "They're really going to let me leave?"

Geneva nodded vigorously. "Yes. Who would have

ever thought a pair of Steller's sea cows would be your salvation?''

Thomas tilted his head and studied her. ''Are you happy about bringing those sea cows here, Geneva?''

''Well, I'd hoped to build a preserve for them in Alaska, but that's out of the question now. Your freedom is what's important. Of course I'm going to let Jase have them.''

''And you're not going to stay behind with them?''

''No.'' Somehow her answer didn't come out as forcefully as she'd wanted, nor did it disguise the regret in her voice.

Thomas's face grew serious. ''Don't even think about it, Geneva. This is a beautiful place, and the people here are kind, but The Sanctuary is not for you. It's been a long time, Geneva, but I still know you. You couldn't stand being cooped up here any more than I could.''

Geneva shifted uneasily on her chair. ''I know I can't stay. But maybe I could come back—you know, to check on the sea cows.'' *And to see Jase again.* ''If Jase is allowed to come and go as he pleases, maybe he could arrange the same for me.''

''*Jase Guardian?* You actually believe he'd do that for you?'' Thomas asked incredulously.

''I— Why not? I've seen him in Florida, not once, but on two separate occasions. He's allowed free access between here and the real world.''

''*He* is,'' Thomas replied. ''The rest of us, guests and guardians alike, aren't allowed such liberal privileges.''

''Jase wouldn't lie to me.''

Thomas sighed. ''No, but he wouldn't necessarily

tell you everything, either. What do you *really know* about him? Or this place?''

"I know enough,'' Geneva replied, not liking the turn this conversation was taking.

"How long have you been here? A few days? Well, I've been here twenty years, sister of mine. For your own good, let me fill you in on a few cold, hard facts. For starters, did you know The Sanctuary gives certain people certain gifts?''

She nodded.

"The gifts have a wide range. They can be anything as simple as an increased ability in the five senses to greater physical strength and agility. Or the ability to feel the ocean currents and tides, and the moon's and sun's effects on them. I myself now have all of these.''

"You, Thomas?''

"Yes. I can swim longer distances, at greater depths and in weather conditions that would drown a normal person.''

Geneva nodded. She herself had seen how long Jase could hold his breath, how fast he could swim, how easily he'd navigated the rough waters surrounding Thomas's island.

"But the other gifts are much more rare. I can't maneuver back and forth through The Sanctuary's barriers. Looking at you, I can see that I'm aging normally.''

"You're aging—''

"I've been here twenty years, Geneva. There aren't that many people here. Some of them look as young now as they did when I was a boy. They don't age right. Again, this is rare.''

Geneva's mind called up a picture of Jase. Strange, but when she tried to guess his real age, she couldn't come up with a figure. His body and face looked fit and at their prime, but his eyes weren't those of a carefree youth.

"Is Jase one of them?"

Thomas nodded. "I'm sure he's one of the lucky ones. In fact, he's the luckiest guardian here. He can talk to all the sea life, you know."

"I know. Can *you,* Thomas?" she asked curiously.

"Of course not! Most guardians communicate only with one species. Only a handful of guardians here can talk to two. Any more than that is nonexistent."

Geneva frowned. That didn't sound right. "But Jase can talk to dolphins and porpoises, turtles, manatees and dugongs...." She stopped listing. "Jase can talk to all of them! I've seen him do it!"

Thomas gave her a telling look. "Doesn't that strike you as a bit unusual, Geneva?"

"Well, no. I thought everyone here could do what Jase does."

"Only because he led you to believe it!" Thomas said impatiently. "Did he tell you he was more powerful than all the other guardians?"

"No."

"I see."

"He didn't exactly lie to me," Geneva defended Jase. "He just—"

"Didn't tell you all the facts," Thomas said. "Did Jase bother to tell you that he's the second-in-command of this place? Did he tell you that he's the Senior Guardian's heir apparent?"

Geneva was shocked.

"I can see that he didn't. That's why Jase can travel back and forth whenever he pleases, Geneva. He's allowed his freedom. Rank does have its privileges,"

Thomas said with a slight smile. "Jase can go to the mainland whenever he wants instead of on rare occasions like everyone else."

"Thomas, I didn't know that…but what difference does it make, anyway?" she asked. "What Jase can and can't do doesn't affect our bargain either way. You get to go free in return for the Steller's sea cows. That was our agreement."

"And The Sanctuary always keeps its bargains," Thomas replied. "But they don't mind if they get a little more for their money. Can't you guess *who* they want for guardian for these sea cows?"

Thomas's pointed look sent a chill down Geneva's spine. "Just what exactly are you saying, Thomas?"

"The Sanctuary wants you to stay, Geneva. A marine biologist like you is valuable property. They'll beg you, bribe you, do anything to get you to stay here. *Anything.*"

Geneva's heart stopped as a horrifying thought stabbed at her chest. Were Jase's actions toward her Sanctuary-ordered? Had his tender words and loving acts disguised an unthinkable ulterior motive?

"I don't believe that." She forced herself to stay calm. "The only interest The Sanctuary has in me professionally is in finding the sea cows."

Her heart was dealt another shattering blow with Thomas's response.

"Geneva, Jase will get his sea cows with or without you. With his powers, he doesn't really need you to find them."

"He does!" she cried.

"He doesn't, Geneva. Use your head! He can talk to any damn thing that swims. Jase can find out the location of any sea creature anywhere on this planet without ever leaving his island. All he needs is the general location, which you conveniently gave him. Jase's wards will ask other wards, and those wards will ask the next sea of wards, and so on. Oh, it might take a while longer without you, but sooner or later Jase will find them.''

''Your theory has one major flaw, Thomas,'' Geneva countered. ''Why would The Sanctuary offer to release you for the sea cows?''

Thomas shrugged. ''They're probably just trying to soften you up and lull you into a false sense of security. They want you to take the pledge, Geneva. There aren't enough guardians to go around. The existing guardians The Sanctuary has come from all walks of life. Sailors and pilots make for very uneducated caretakers. But an honest-to-God marine biologist such as yourself... Don't you see, Geneva? They want you just as much as they want the sea cows.''

''I don't believe it. I *won't* believe it!''

Thomas sighed. ''Maybe I'm wrong. But you should know all the facts before you make up your mind. Don't let The Sanctuary's particular brand of magic cloud your judgment. It's a beautiful place here, and the people are good, but those who pledge are bound by ironclad rules. Rules a visitor like you can't expect to learn in a few short days. You'll be trapped here just as surely as I've been.''

Geneva shivered, some of the joy at meeting her brother fading. Could the man she was falling in love with more and more each day be suspect?

Thomas seemed to sense her despair, and he hugged her tight. ''I'm sorry, Geneva. I didn't mean to ruin our reunion, but I thought you should know.''

''Jase has been very good to me, Thomas,'' Geneva

forced herself to say in an even voice. "I can't believe he'd lie to me."

Thomas studied her for a long while. Geneva tried to hide the truth from him, but their "twin thing" was working well. Her feelings for Jase were as obvious to Thomas as his sympathy and concern was for her.

"It's easy enough to prove, Sis," Thomas said gently. "Ask him if he's the second-in-command here. Ask him how many others can talk to *all* the sea creatures. Ask him if he already knows where your sea cows are. Love him as much as you want. But remember, his first loyalty will always be to The Sanctuary, Geneva. Never you."

They sat in silence for a long time, their arms around each other. Suddenly Thomas lifted his head as a young woman peered into the room and gestured. Thomas nodded in acknowledgement, then kissed his sister on the cheek.

"Jase is waiting, Geneva. It's time for you to go."

Geneva rose to her feet. She even managed to give her twin a wide smile. "I promise I'll be back for you, Thomas. Just as soon as I bring the sea cows here."

"I'll be waiting." Thomas gave her one last hug. "Be very careful while you're here in The Sanctuary, twin. Remember…even paradise had its serpent."

Geneva was deeply troubled by his parting words as Thomas walked her halfway back to the beach. He left her as soon as Jase emerged from the rough surf. She stared at Jase for a long time, emotions washing over her like the fierce breakers on the rocks. Had the love they'd exchanged been just a cruel sham? Had she given herself to a man worthy of her trust? Or was Jase Guardian part of The Sanctuary's plan to lure her here forever?

"We have to go, Geneva."

She looked up, startled to see Jase at her side.

"There's a storm brewing."

Geneva shivered as he touched her arm and drew her into the raging waters. She couldn't help a backward glance toward Thomas's retreating figure.

"You'll see him again," Jase promised. "We have to go," he repeated, guiding her into the water.

The fury of the sea was all around as the dolphins and their master encircled her. She felt Jase's arm around her waist, felt his sudden surge of strength as he and his escorts overpowered the currents and cleared the rocks. Felt him carry her onto the deck of his wildly tossing boat, down below and gently wrap her in blankets.

"We're being dragged to the shore. I have to go topside now, Geneva, or we'll founder on the rocks. Are you going to be all right?"

Geneva didn't answer. Didn't *dare* speak, for if she opened her mouth, all the questions she wanted to ask him would come tumbling out. And right now, she couldn't bear to hear his answers.

"Geneva?"

She turned away from him. Jase remained a few seconds longer, then sighed, a sigh Geneva heard even above the howling wind and the waves smashing into the side of the boat. Then he was gone.

She heard the reassuring sound of the boat motor, saw the flash of delphine escorts through her porthole and watched Thomas's island grow smaller in the distance.

She'd never felt more alone in her life.

"YOU CAN HAVE the Steller's sea cows," Geneva announced. "They're yours."

Jase swung around in surprise at the sound of her voice. Geneva hadn't spoken a word to him since yesterday. They'd barely made it back to the shelter of his island before the full fury of the storm broke. Through the violent pitching and yawing of his boat, she'd been deathly still.

Even when they'd made the shore, raced through the torrential rain and reached the safety of his bungalow, she remained mute. And she had continued that way throughout the rest of the night. For Jase, her silence was agony. He couldn't stand their sudden estrangement and was certain that somehow Geneva's twin was the root of her withdrawal.

He wished she would say something, anything, but there was nothing. So they sat out the storm in silence while he watched her with a strange stitch in his heart. Then he'd retired to his hammock, alone. She'd retired to hers, alone, the sudden gulf between them yawning like an ocean cavern. And now it was the next morning.

"You have the Steller's sea cows. They're yours."

"Geneva..." Although this was what he'd sought from the very beginning, he felt no surge of triumph.

Geneva didn't let him finish his sentence. "I've already packed. I'm ready to go whenever you are."

"So soon? Don't you want to stay awhile longer? There's so much I wanted to show you! And you've barely visited with your brother."

He abruptly broke off, not wanting her to think he was pleading. *Which he was.* The thought of being alone again here at The Sanctuary was agony. Her coming had shone the harsh light of reality on his solitary existence. He'd never be content with it again.

"I want to leave," she said in an expressionless voice.

"As you wish." Jase turned away from her, his chest tight. "I'll get the boat."

The sun shone brightly as they shoved off, burning away the last traces of the storm. Jase's wards were happily riding the waves at the bow, their high spirits a contrast to the mood on board. The craft's two people showed no joy in the brilliance of the morning or the beauty of the calm turquoise sea.

Jase watched Geneva from the flying bridge. She stood alone at the bow, watching his dolphins with dispassionate eyes. Her hair hung down her back in one long braid, her body was clothed in the same slacks and sweater she'd worn on the trip out. As for her face, he couldn't tell what expression it wore. Since climbing aboard, not once had she looked in his direction.

Finally Jase could stand it no longer. He set the controls on autopilot and climbed down to the deck. He stood next to the railing she was leaning against, refusing to keep a discreet, tactful distance between them. Still she refused to look at him. It wasn't until he moved next to her, his shirtless shoulder touching hers, that she was forced to acknowledge his presence.

"Is it time for me to drink your drugged coffee?" she asked listlessly.

"We still have a few minutes before that becomes necessary." Jase hooked his thumbs into his jeans pockets. "What's wrong, Geneva?"

Geneva turned back toward the water and was silent. For a long time the two of them watched his wards. Pacific spotted dolphins, spinner dolphins and harbor porpoises had joined his usual schools of Commersons and bottle-nose. All were vying for the choice positions closest to the bow, the competition fiercely exuberant.

When she finally did answer, it was to remark, "It's so strange to see the schools mix together. You rarely see that unless there's a rich food supply."

"Sanctuary wards who share the same guardian have a special bond with one another," he replied. "And you still haven't answered my question."

Geneva finally met his gaze. "Why didn't you tell me about yourself?"

"Geneva, you know I don't like to talk about my former life."

"I mean your Sanctuary life! You haven't told me about that, either!" she cried. "Why didn't you tell me you were only one of two guardians who could talk to all the marine life?"

"Your brother told you?"

At Geneva's nod, Jase wasn't surprised. Thomas Kelsey was an extremely intelligent man. He might not be able to communicate with the sea life, but he'd learned much in his twenty years in The Sanctuary.

"Is it true, Jase?"

"Yes."

"Why did you let me think it was a common, ordinary thing? Or that *you* were a common, ordinary man here?"

Jase sighed. "Because I didn't want you to be any more frightened of me than you already were. And you *were* frightened, Geneva. Later, after you began to trust me, it didn't seem to matter."

A bottle-nose jumped high in the air, close enough

to the bow that Jase could have touched it if he wanted. He didn't. His attention was focused wholly on Geneva.

"Are you really the heir apparent to The Sanctuary, like Thomas says?"

Jase thought about that. It was a subject the Senior Guardian had never brought up directly. Still, the assumption was always there. "I've never really asked, but probably."

"Did the Senior Guardian order you to convince me to stay here?"

"Yes. Not only are you valuable as a marine biologist, but I think he suspects I care for you. Very much."

At Geneva's soft indrawn gasp of air, he pulled her into his arms. "Geneva, listen to me. No one plays matchmaker for me, *ever*. I prefer to choose my own woman."

Geneva lifted shining eyes to his. "Really, Jase?"

"Really, Geneva." Jase smiled. "So that's what this is all about. You think I'm guilty of the same thing I once accused you of? Using my charms for ulterior motives?"

"Thomas thought so," Geneva reluctantly admitted. "I didn't really believe him," she said, laying her head on his shoulder and allowing him to stroke her hair. "But I wanted to be sure."

"You can be sure. Can I help it if the Senior Guardian's taste in women just happens to coincide with mine?" The smile faded from his face as he asked the question he'd been burning to ask. "Do you think you could stay here in The Sanctuary? With me?"

"Oh, Jase…" Geneva lifted her head to meet his gaze. "How could I? I have work, important work, on the mainland. And family and friends. And Thomas. Jase, Thomas doesn't want to stay here! I don't think I could bear for us to be separated again. I need him, and he needs me!''

Her eyes were troubled. ''He hasn't been to school since he was fifteen. He hasn't seen a VCR, a computer, a shuttle launch, anything. Thomas isn't equipped to hold down a normal job, and he doesn't have a cent to his name. Who else but me could help him adjust to the real world again?''

''What about us, Geneva?''

''Can't you come with me?'' Geneva pleaded.

''I can't. My life is in The Sanctuary now.''

''And I can't stay, Jase!''

''Then what do we do?'' Jase asked in a voice rough with emotion.

''We make the most of the time we have left.''

Jase gathered her close again, and they stood in each other's embrace. Jase could have remained that way forever, but that was not to be. His Sanctuary senses kicked in and warned him that he had little time left.

''Ten minutes before we hit the barriers, Geneva. We need to get back to the bridge.''

She didn't acknowledge his words, but he knew she'd heard him. Reluctantly she left his embrace. With none of the customary grace he usually associated with her, she made her way up to the flying bridge. He followed.

The fog began to roll in at the same time most of his wards turned and headed back toward his island. The few remaining dolphins and porpoises tightened formation, their sonar activity increasing as visibility lessened and the skies darkened. Jase saw Geneva lift her head at the first flash of noiseless lightning.

Jase had the coffee, and the small vial of colorless liquid waiting. Wordlessly he handed both to her. Geneva didn't bother with the thermos. She drank the sleeping potion straight, handed him back the vial and headed for the ladder. Jase's arm reached for her waist to stop her departure.

"Forget the berth, Geneva. Stay with me."

Geneva looked at him and nodded. He knew she was thinking the same thing. *We have so little time left.*

Jase sat down in the captain's chair he rarely used and gathered her into his lap. He placed her back against his chest, one arm fast around her waist, the other on the ship's wheel. He tucked her head under his chin and held her tight.

Geneva's eyes were still open. She and Jase watched the dolphins leap as he gently smoothed back her spray-soaked bangs. He felt her body relax as her hand slid down his chest and fell limply onto his thigh. Her eyes closed, then fluttered open again at a sudden thought.

"Jase, how hard is it to get through the barriers?"

Jase thought about that. "Not hard at all, once you figure out the barrier pattern. That's the difficult part—learning to recognize it. The barrier elements shift and change from month to month, but the basic pattern remains the same."

"Do you think you could teach me?"

"Teach you?"

Geneva nodded. "Yes. If I learned the way, maybe I could come and visit you."

Jase fought against the temptation that surged through his veins at her suggestion. He fought so hard, in fact, that his voice was harsh when he replied, "It's not permitted, Geneva. Not ever."

"Why? Can't the Capulets ever mix with the Montagues?"

Jase refused to give in to the urgent plea in her voice. "Geneva, compared to us, Romeo and Juliet had it easy." His eyes gazed out into the eerie ocean before them. "They never had to deal with The Sanctuary."

Geneva shuddered just once, and was silent. A few minutes later her body grew totally limp in his arms. The sky grew darker and darker, and the fog grew thick. Jase was forced to stand, holding an unconscious Geneva in one arm and steering with the other, for the sea was now fierce. He mentally checked on his remaining wards and was startled at their cries of surprise.

The Senior Guardian's schooner? Off the port side?

Excited agreement filled his mind.

What does he want?

A pause, a response, then Jase's reply for them to relay.

Yes, the woman saw her brother. Yes, she's agreed to our demands. Yes, we're leaving for Alaska.

The message was transmitted, along with the dolphins' regret at his departure.

The Senior Guardian will watch after you, as he always does when I'm away. Soon I'll be back. I always come back, he reassured them.

There was another pause as his wards assimilated that. Then another message.

The Senior Guardian wants me to put my mate below? Tell him she's drugged. She can see nothing, learn nothing. No, she won't get cold. I'll keep her warm. Tell the Senior Guardian I'll protect her with my life.

His wards transmitted. Jase grimaced as they relayed to him the older man's return message. It was a question, and one he didn't wish to answer.

Tell him…because I wish to hold her. Why? Just… because. Because. Because.

The dolphins were confused at the ambiguity of his message, but at his urging they relayed it, anyway. There was no response, nor did he expect one. Jase watched as the schooner heeled high in the water, sails flapping as it turned away from the barrier's fog banks. Within minutes the gusting wind was at the departing schooner's back.

Because…

Because Jase wanted Geneva in his arms. She filled a gaping hole in him that he'd never known how to fill, how to heal. But that hole had become smaller every time he'd touched her, every time he held her. And those moments would soon end.

Because with all his Sanctuary powers, even he couldn't stop time. So, like now, he treasured every moment he spent with her. Even moments like these.

Because they were all he had.

Chapter Ten

The Florida sun was directly overhead as Jase docked in Miami. Much to his satisfaction, a car and driver were waiting for him at the end of the pier. The driver came over and made fast the lines to Jase's boat, then silently went below deck to retrieve Jase's and Geneva's bags. Jase didn't know the driver's name, nor did he bother to ask. Each of the men had their own jobs to do.

Jase carefully descended the flying bridge with the unconscious Geneva. The driver stood at the bottom of the ladder and waited for Jase to lower Geneva to him, but Jase shook his head. He wouldn't entrust her to anyone but himself.

With a shrug, the driver then went to open up the back door of the limo for Jase. A few minutes later the boat was secured, humans and cargo were safely stowed, and the limo was off.

The driver lowered the clear partition between chauffeur and passenger, reached into his glove compartment and passed Jase an envelope.

"Open it," Jase commanded, the first words he'd spoken since Geneva had lost consciousness. He shifted her to a more comfortable position in his arms, her legs stretched out on the long seat, her body in his lap, her head on his shoulder. ''Give me the contents.''

The driver complied.

Jase took the sheaf of papers and studied it. Included were an itinerary of the private plane chartered to fly them to Alaska, a list of the supplies awaiting him on his arrival, including his and hers arctic winter gear and the location of the craft made available for his use in the polar waters. There was also a line of credit provided for him in the city of Nome.

Jase handed the papers back to the driver, who refolded them, stuffed them back in the envelope and gave the reassembled packet to Jase. Having discarded his shirt and jacket, Jase put the packet in one of the limo's spacious storage pockets. Dressed in jeans and nothing else, he planned to change on the plane, knowing that shoes and a change of clothes, all tailor-made for a perfect fit, would be waiting for him. He was about to settle back for the ride when the driver spoke.

''Left seat pocket.''

Jase leaned over and retrieved the contents of the pocket, holding tightly to Geneva as her weight shifted in his arms. Inside was a medical packet holding an antidote dose.

He replaced the packet untouched. Jase wouldn't risk giving her an injection in a moving vehicle. He'd wait until after the short ride to the airport. He saw the driver's nod in the mirror, then listened as the driver spoke his longest speech yet.

''Can't say I blame you. It'll make things easier to wait.''

Jase looked down at the pale face cradled above his arm. Easy? Wasting what little time they had left together like this?

Something in Jase's demeanor caused the driver to nervously take his eyes off the mirror and concentrate on the road. There was no more conversation on the way to the airport.

The private jet was new, plush and equipped with all the modern conveniences, including a sleeping cabin. Jase made certain Geneva was settled in the narrow bed, then securely belted in for takeoff before he administered the antidote. It wasn't until he was satisfied with her comfort and had checked her pulse one last time that he signaled the plane's attendant that he was ready for takeoff.

Once in the air, he dressed himself in the outfit laid out for him on the opposite bed, then signaled the attendant once more.

"Could we please turn up the heat in here," he asked a gray-haired, matronly woman. "And maybe get another blanket, please. I don't want her getting chilled."

"Sure, sir. Is there anything else?"

"I'd like something to eat—beef if you've got it, poultry if not. Anything but fish."

"Yes, sir," the woman replied, already on her way out the door. "Sir? Will the young lady be joining you for lunch?"

He paused, studying the slight movements on the bed.

"She certainly will," he said with a satisfied smile.

"How much longer before we land?" Geneva asked.

She sat cross-legged on the bed, a blanket wrapped around her shoulders, a bowl of hot soup before her. She'd been awake for some time now.

Her first glimpse of consciousness had been Jase's face. Remembering the last time she'd been given the antidote, she'd remained still and followed his orders. Her compliance had paid off. The disorientation was gone, the side effects had been minimal and she was actually eating.

Not that she had much of an appetite under the circumstances. Geneva remembered every word of their conversation at the barriers. She still couldn't accept the fact that eventually they'd each have to go their separate ways. But she refused to give into depression over that inevitable fact. There would be plenty of time for that later. For now, she intended to live in the present, which meant forcing herself to continue eating.

She even managed a cheerful tone to her voice when she asked when they would land.

"In little over an hour," Jase replied. "Are you getting anxious?"

"Excited," she corrected him. "We're finally going to get the sea cows. What arrangements have you made for them?"

She listened as Jase filled her in on the boat and supplies waiting.

"We should have everything we need upon landing," he concluded. "I've decided on a sea transport back to The Sanctuary. What with the water volume we'll need to fill transport tanks, I think a sea transport would be easier going than by air. I've got the plans drawn up here if you want to take a look."

"I will later, thanks." Geneva suddenly frowned. "We may need some more people to help—and I don't want the press in on this."

"All our help has been arranged through the Senior

Guardian. You have nothing to worry about.'' Jase stood up and took her dishes. ''I'll send the attendant in with your clothes. You'll need to get out of those summer clothes before we land. When you're done changing, join me out front.''

Geneva was glad when both he and the flight attendant were gone and she was left alone. She needed time to think, to plan, and to get her turbulent emotions under control.

She didn't want to leave Jase. But the alternative— a life sentence in The Sanctuary—was beyond comprehension. How could she be longing for the impossible?

The disadvantages were many. She'd be torn away from her work, her home, her family and Thomas. But she'd be among rare and supposedly extinct animals. And Jase would be there....

She'd have Jase, her heart whispered.

Jase Guardian. *Who was he really?* He was as secretive about his Sanctuary life as he was about his previous life in the real world. She vowed anew to continue her efforts to learn who Jase Guardian had once been. But not now. That was for later, when she was settled back in her old routine...without Jase.

Geneva cringed at even the thought of the loneliness waiting for her. She resolutely pushed it to the back of her mind, then changed and rejoined Jase. He stood up as she approached.

''Do the clothes fit all right?'' he asked, gesturing for her to take a seat next to him on the jet's spacious couch.

''Yes, thank you.'' Geneva fingered the turtleneck of the expensive cashmere top. ''They're quite comfortable, and exactly the right size.''

Jase's eyes gleamed with amusement. "They never get it wrong."

"They?"

"Sanctuary travel agents."

"You'll have to give me their phone number someday," she said with a smile. "I'm definitely getting spoiled by them." She dropped her hand from the collar and sat down next to him. "Did you get a weather report, Jase?"

"Clear skies, calm seas. The temperature's in the high forties, about average, I'm told."

Geneva nodded. Fifty-five degrees was about as hot as it got during Nome summers.

"Did you get the water temperature?"

"We won't need it."

"Of course we will! Jase, this isn't Florida! Even with dry suits specially made for the arctic, we wouldn't be able to stay in the water for long. Just how are we supposed to trap these creatures? Whistle them into the boat?"

"Something like that." At Geneva's look of confusion, Jase pursed his lips and whistled, his eyes mocking her. "Surely you haven't forgotten, Geneva?"

Geneva crossed her arms against her chest, feeling slightly foolish and more than a little envious. "Dr. Doolittle strikes again. Obviously my tried-and-true scientific methods of capture aren't going to be needed on *this* expedition."

"Don't feel bad, Geneva." Jase leaned over and kissed her cheek. "My way will be less of a strain on the two sea cows than yours would be."

"I hope so. I don't want anything to happen to them."

"Everything will go as planned. And I, for one, am sick of talking shop." Jase pulled Geneva onto his lap. "I can think of better things to do with my time."

"Jase!" Geneva felt his hands slowly travel up her sides, his palms warm and welcoming. Her eyes opened wide as she saw desire spark in his. "Not on an airplane!" she whispered.

"Don't be so conventional, Dr. Kelsey." Jase kissed her neck, then trailed a string of kisses down her shoulder. "You didn't mind loving me on a beach. Or in the water…"

Geneva looked anxiously toward the cockpit containing the jet's two pilots and attendant, even as she shivered beneath his touch. "Yes, but there we didn't have an audience," she protested.

"We won't be disturbed," he assured her. "They'll only come out if I call them. We can go to the back room where you changed, if you want."

"It wouldn't make any difference," Geneva said, and sighed with real regret. "It'll still be like necking on my aunt's front porch while she waited up for me inside. Talk about inhibition city. Not to mention the time limit," she groaned. "We'll be landing soon."

"The real world always did have too many complications." Jase's face held a touch of bitterness.

"I'm sorry, Jase. I guess there's a lot to be said for deserted islands, after all." She gave him a quick, apologetic kiss. "Let me look at those transport plans you told me about," she suggested.

Jase handed her the file, then watched as she quietly studied its contents. Geneva may have calmly accepted that their relationship was to be a here-and-now affair, but deep down inside, he hadn't. More than anything, he wanted to convince her to stay in the The Sanctuary.

You've done a great job of convincing her so far, Jase thought with disgust as Geneva pored over the file.

Still, there was time. She might be able to resist him now, but once they were at sea, he'd have the advantage then. There, he was in his true element. Jase loved the ocean and its creatures with a fierceness he knew Geneva shared. He knew she'd envied his special powers ever since he'd correctly diagnosed Marnee's uterine infection—an infection Geneva had missed.

Perhaps he could use that in his favor. He could share one of his gifts with her when they reached the Steller's sea cows—on a temporary basis, of course. It was quite obvious that Geneva Kelsey couldn't be charmed into changing her mind.

But maybe, just maybe, she could be bribed....

THE ALASKAN MORNING was crisp and clear as Jase helped Geneva out of the limo that had driven them to the harbor. There was no snow on the ground, but already the mountains in the distance had white peaks. The breath of snow was in the air.

"Where's our transport? We can't go hunting sea cows on *this*," Geneva argued as Jase led her to the waiting motorboat. "What are we supposed to do when we find them? Tow them south?"

"I hadn't thought of that." Jase pretended to take her outlandish suggestion seriously just to enjoy her reaction.

"Steller's sea cows are twenty-six feet long! That's longer than this boat!"

Jase smiled. "This isn't our sea-cow-catching craft,

Geneva. That is.'' He pointed out toward the huge ship anchored offshore. At Geneva's gasp, he laughed aloud and helped her aboard the smaller vessel. "She's too big for the pier, so we'll just motor on out. If you have no complaints about the size, that is.''

"I have *got* to meet this Sanctuary travel agent!" Geneva gasped. "I've seen cruise ships that are smaller!" She took another look at their vessel. "You know, for a man who runs around half naked, you sure do like to travel first class.''

Geneva continued to stare at the ship as she cast off. "How in the world did you pay for it? Don't tell me The Sanctuary has buried treasure, after all?''

"Nope." Jase started the engines and flipped the switch to lift anchor. "But we do make certain sales to the public from time to time.''

"Sales? You mean—you sell your rare *animals?*''

Jase laughed at the shocked expression on her face. He'd laughed more with Geneva Kelsey than he had in the past five years. "Museums are *so* gullible," he explained with a wink. "Where do you think that dead prehistoric coelacanth fish you biologists thought was extinct came from?" He shook his head in mock dismay. "And everyone thought some old fisherman had found it in his net.''

"That's—that's dishonest!''

"Nope. The coelacanth was the genuine article that died a natural death, and was only too happy to contribute to the cause." Jase gestured toward the transport ship.

Geneva looped up the last of the lines. "So that's how you pay for frills like these?''

"Not frills. Necessary expenses needed for our conservation efforts," Jason corrected her as he idled away from the pier. "Haven't you read about fishermen who just 'happen' to come across a rare sea creature? Or an animal lover who just 'happens' to come across a bird that had supposedly been wiped out of its natural habitat?"

"You mean…"

Jase nodded. "That's us. The scenarios are carefully orchestrated and paid for. Hey, it worked for the California condors and the whooping cranes. We transported a few from The Sanctuary to people we can trust in the real world. They pass these animals on to the zoos to get a breeding colony going."

"I know you told me your land space was limited."

"Even if it wasn't, conservation efforts cost money, whether in The Sanctuary or not. We have to finance our work some way, Geneva."

"I suppose. Jase…"

"Yes?" Jase increased his speed as they moved away from the heavier boat traffic and out toward the open water where the ship was anchored.

"How are we going to get the sea cows to the holding tanks below deck? The cows are at least two metric tons each. They're massive."

"I've taken that into account. Once we flood the ship's holding tanks with seawater and make certain the food and temperature levels are correct, we'll transport the cows via a specially adapted crane through an oversize cargo hatch."

"This ship is equipped with all that?"

"Hey, we've got stuff here Jacques Cousteau would envy. Better yet, it's all tax free."

"Tax free?" Geneva shaded her eyes and peered off into the distance. "What flag do we sail under?" she asked curiously.

"Whatever's most convenient at the time. Customs can be a big problem when it comes to animals. It's easier to avoid them at sea than in the air, so we avoid airports whenever possible, and switch flags and registration papers on our crafts quite often."

"You cheat customs?" Geneva exclaimed.

Jase gave her a telling look. "When it comes to protecting our rare animals, yes. That includes keeping our wards out of primitive customs holding facilities. More smuggled exotic animals—especially parrots—die in foreign facilities than at the hands of the smugglers," he informed her. "So we don't feel guilty at all ignoring the law."

Geneva considered that. "Does ignoring the law include stealing smuggled rare animals from customs?"

Jase shrugged. "That's not my line of work. However, the people who work for The Sanctuary are quite adept at making the most of any opportunities."

"Between your pledges and rules and hidden location, you make it sound like a cloak-and-dagger operation," Geneva said lightly. "Next you'll be showing me your secret decoder ring and whispering passwords in my ear."

"This is nothing to joke about, Geneva," Jase replied tersely. "I've learned that playing by the rules doesn't always work when it comes to the real world."

Geneva gave him a sad smile, her face framed by the hood of her parka. "Nor in The Sanctuary, either, Jase. We're a prime example of that."

Jase didn't say a word, but his gloved hand reached for hers as the little craft continued on its journey.

The crew of the *Star of the Sea* was on hand to help Jase and Geneva aboard. As their gear and supplies had been stowed away earlier, the ship immediately got underway as soon as the smaller transport boat turned toward the pier.

Jase started for the bridge, his arm linked through Geneva's.

"Where are we headed?" she asked. "Our quarters?"

"No, to the bridge. I'm the captain of this vessel."

"You?"

"Yes. Except for the Senior Guardian's schooner, I command *all* Sanctuary vessels."

Geneva brushed back her bangs, obviously impressed by Jase's announcement. Her parka hood had fallen and lay halfway back on her head. Jase resisted an urge to push it all the way down to her shoulders and expose that slender, graceful neck.

"Well, Captain, if you'll take me to your chart room, I'll show you the course to plot to find the sea cows."

"That won't be necessary. I've already laid in a course."

"But, Jase, how will you find them without my—" Her voice broke off abruptly as he allowed the answer to her question to show on his face. "Don't tell me you know where they are already?"

Jase lifted his chin in acknowledgement. "I do. I located them shortly after the plane landed."

Geneva actually stopped in her tracks. "But we were nowhere near the water!"

"I was busy right after we landed at the airport."

"But you said you have to have direct contact with a new species for the first meeting!"

"True. But I didn't talk to the sea cows. I talked to some sea lions instead. They feed in the same kelp forests as the cows and were able to give me the location."

"Oh."

Jase smiled as the wind was taken out of Geneva's sails. "I know you want to help, but everything's under control. I won't need your expertise until later, Geneva."

"And you'll certainly get it," she replied in an even voice. "Although I must confess to feeling somewhat useless on this excursion so far," she said ruefully.

"Don't underestimate yourself, Geneva." His hand dropped to the small of her back and he urged her forward. "You're more valuable than you realize."

UNDER JASE'S COMMAND, the *Star of the Sea* was set to sail around the Seward Peninsula through the Bering Strait and into the Chukchi Sea. Although the original population of Steller's sea cows had inhabited the remote Aleutian chain of Alaska, the remaining two survivors had moved toward the greater protection of the icy seas farther north.

Jase easily made contact with three different species of arctic sea mammals. They all confirmed that the sea cows were wintering off of Point Hope, a nautical distance of 750 miles, and a mere two days' journey for the powerful engines of the *Star of the Sea*. Calm seas and clear skies allowed the ship to make good time, while the experienced crew and crackerjack first officer needed little supervision.

On the first day of their journey Jase and Geneva went over the holding area, Geneva worked on making improvements to the original setup. They worked long into the night and fell into the captain's narrow bed exhausted. Both were asleep in minutes, yet early the next morning they were up before sunrise to check out the diving equipment, and the crane and nets to be used for capture.

That task took all day. By late evening, the two of them were still on the job formulating a dive plan.

"We're agreed, then?" Jase said, shoving his copy of the dive schedule her way. "This should work?"

Geneva pushed back an errant strand of hair, her elbows resting on the small table in the captain's quarters.

"It'll only work if you can get the sea cows up to the shallower water. I don't want a dive where we have to decompress, and we can only do that if we don't go deep. As it is, we'll only be able to dive ten to twelve minutes max in these frigid waters."

"The cows will come to me. We won't have to decompress," Jase assured her. "But it'll probably take longer than that to get them safely netted and ready for the crane."

Geneva bit her lip and tapped her pencil. "We could do two dives, one morning and one afternoon, and do one cow at a time."

Jase shook his head. "I don't want to risk separation anxiety. They'll be under enough stress as it is. We'll do them one right after the other. I can stay in the water up to twenty minutes. That should be long enough."

"You'll get hypothermia!" she protested.

"I won't. I once told you I can stand temperature extremes longer than you, remember?" He warmed to her troubled look of concern and reached for her hand. "Nothing will happen to me, Geneva. We'll reach Point Hope before dawn tomorrow. If the weather holds, we'll dive as soon as the light's good."

"So soon?"

"Yes, I'm afraid so."

Geneva gave him a rueful look. "If I'd known that, I would have made certain I didn't fall asleep on you last night."

"Unfortunately, I was right behind you." Jase left his chair to place his hands on her shoulders and kissed the top of her head. "But since we have to dive tomorrow, we really should just concentrate on getting a good night's rest tonight, too," he said reluctantly.

Geneva gave him a warning look. "You do, and I'll be sending complaints instead of compliments to your travel agent."

"Hey, I'm only concerned with your welfare. You know fatigue and diving never mix, especially in frigid waters."

Geneva rose from her chair and turned in his arms to face him. "If you were *really* concerned with my welfare…" She trailed her fingers down his chest with obvious intent.

Jase gave her a slow, sensuous look. "Aren't you happy with the service?"

"No, I'm not. In fact—" Geneva reached for the buttons on his wool shirt "—I might have to personally complain to the captain."

He pulled Geneva to her feet and led her to their narrow bunk. "I have a feeling he'll be most attentive."

JASE ROSE BEFORE THE SUN, but Geneva was up even earlier. He found her below, doing a last precheck on the dive equipment and holding tanks. In arctic waters, dry suits that repelled water were needed instead of the traditional neoprene wet suits. He quietly watched her work until she finally noticed his presence.

"Good morning," Jase said, hating the bulky arctic clothing that hid her from both his eyes and his touch.

Geneva gave him a welcoming kiss. "Hello, Jase."

She retrieved their dive computers from the storage lockers and proceeded to scroll the screens, checking to see that all displays were functional. Jase watched her finish with the dive computer and begin with the compass.

"You're down here awfully early," he observed.

"I know. I woke up early and couldn't get back to sleep." She held the compass level, checking to see that the magnetic needle swiveled freely.

"Too excited?"

"Not exactly."

Geneva didn't elaborate. She set down the computer, then checked out the straps on the sheath of the knife all wise divers carried. It wasn't only marine animals who became trapped in the near-invisible, practically unbreakable monofilament fishing nets. Divers could become enmeshed, too.

"The equipment is top of the line. Besides, I went over all of it late last night."

Geneva looked up at him in confusion. "You, Jase?"

"Yes. I didn't sleep very well, either," he admitted. He joined her, putting the equipment back in storage. "I kept thinking about the sea cows," he said quietly. "And how once we had them, we wouldn't have each other."

Geneva's brown eyes were pensive. "The prospect of saying goodbye didn't make for a very comfortable night for me, either," she admitted.

Jase closed the locker doors and faced her. "It's not too late to change your mind, Geneva. About staying in The Sanctuary with me."

"Oh, Jase, we've been over this before," Geneva said impatiently. "We decided no strings...no regrets."

Jase shook his head. "*You* decided. And I don't think I can go along with the no-regret part."

"You have no choice. I have no choice." Geneva abruptly turned on her heel and headed toward the topside ladder.

Jase raced after her and pulled her hard against his chest. He kissed her, putting all his want, his need, his love, on the line for her to feel.

Geneva didn't respond as he had hoped. "Jase, you're only making a bad situation worse," she said, her eyes dark with emotion. "Please let me go. I have work to do."

Jase's grip around her tightened. "I won't. Not until you know what you're throwing away!"

"Damn it, Jase, don't you think I *know?*"

"No, Sweet Survivor, you don't know the *half* of it...."

Then his mouth was hard on hers again. He filled his mind with thoughts of Geneva and thoughts of The Sanctuary, and concentrated.

And concentrated...until the Steller's sea cows that filled his mind filled hers, too.

Jase knew instantly when the connection between Geneva and the sirenians began, because she immediately stopped fighting him. Her mouth opened in surprise as a tiny gasp escaped. He deepened her connection to the cows even as he deepened his kiss, his tongue gently probing as he allowed Geneva's mind to gently probe the sea cows' brains.

He felt her body shake with excitement, fiercely glad he was the one who put it there, fiercely angry that it was the sea cows that held her interest, not him.

And still he deepened the connection between Geneva and the cows, until finally Geneva was on the same level of communication as he was. Until she finally understood and transmitted at the same high capacity as he did. He felt her sharp, indrawn gasp of air, then her chest was motionless as she reveled in the experience.

"Must I always remind you to breathe around sea creatures?" he murmured tenderly into her mouth, remembering when he'd dived with her manatees at the pier. "Breathe, Geneva."

She nodded. The motion broke the kiss. Before Jase could reinitiate, she spoke.

"I can *feel* them! I can *hear* them! It's—it's not like talking, but I understand them." She brought one trembling hand up to her mouth. "Oh, my God, Jase! Can they understand *me*?"

Jase smiled and gently smoothed back her long bangs. Geneva permitted his caress in stunned silence. Her anguish of earlier was gone. The sparkle in her eyes, the animation in her face, the beauty he loved to see; it was all back.

"Yes, my sweet. They can."

"But Jase, we haven't even seen the Steller's sea cows yet! You said you had to be in direct contact for a first connection!"

"That's true. It's always been that way before. But somehow you've augmented my powers when it comes to sirenians."

"Me?" Geneva asked incredulously. "But I'm not a guardian! Jase, I don't understand."

"I don't, either." He gave her a loving smile. "I can't really explain it, because nothing like this—nothing like *you*—has ever happened to me before. I only know I can do this with you, because of you."

Geneva's face shone with rapture. "And you're actually sharing your powers with me. It's like a dream come true."

"Not exactly," Jase qualified, his fingers still toying with her hair. "Since we're not in The Sanctuary, your powers are restricted. This condition is only temporary, and there are limits attached."

"Limits?" she echoed, the sparkle in her eyes dimming just a bit.

"Yes. You have to be touching me for it to work. Watch."

He reluctantly released her and stepped back a few paces. Immediately he felt the connection weaken. The shocked expression on Geneva's face corresponded exactly with the moment when her connection died.

"It's gone. Oh, Jase, bring it back!" she begged.

Jase opened his arms to her and waited. Without a moment's hesitation she rushed back to him, her own arms encircling his neck.

"I can feel it again!" Her eyes glowed with wonder. "I can hear them again. Jase, they *know* me!"

"Of course they do." Jase smiled and adjusted her more comfortably against his thighs. "I told them all about you, Dr. Kelsey." He traced one of her high cheekbones with his forefinger. "Now do you understand what you'll be giving up when you leave me? And Geneva, there's so much more in The Sanctuary."

"Jase, why didn't you tell me it could be like this?" Geneva lifted her face to his, her mind once again entwined with the Steller's sea cows.

"Because you have to feel it to believe it."

He tenderly watched her surprise and delight. A smile curved his lips as Jase remembered the excitement of his own "first time." He'd been swimming in the lagoon, lost in his painful thoughts of the past, when he heard the dominant male bottle-nose dolphin in his head. Jase had choked on seawater, he'd been so surprised. By the time he'd caught his breath and realized what had happened, the delphine-human connection was complete. And blissfully, ecstatically permanent.

Of course, there had been other times with other species, until one by one all the creatures of the sea were his wards. But nothing had ever matched that special, precious first time with the dolphins. He was glad he was there to see Geneva's joy and share in it.

And hope that maybe she might reconsider and stay with him in The Sanctuary forever...

Jase stood there for a long time, taking pleasure in her joy. It wasn't until another Sanctuary power of his was activated that he moved away from Geneva again, breaking her connection with the sea cows.

"Jase?" She took an eager step toward him, her enthusiasm hard for Jase to refuse. But he did.

"Don't touch me," he ordered in a voice that brooked no disobedience.

"No more?" Her disappointment was acute, but she obeyed.

"No, Geneva. We have to dive. I feel a need to hurry."

"What's wrong?"

Jase concentrated and didn't like what he felt. "We're due for a weather change. *Soon.* In fact, let's get suited now and on deck. I'll notify the crew."

Geneva nodded. She followed his directions to the letter and continued to do so, even in the water. Despite her expertise with the arctic conditions, her knowledge of Alaska's ocean didn't surpass his. But neither did his surpass hers. Jase realized that Geneva Kelsey was his equal. His powers made him safe, but her knowledge and experience gave her the same buffer of protection. The two of them worked like well-oiled machinery.

Jase called for the sea cows before hitting the water, for both his and Geneva's time in the frigid sea was limited. The sirenians were close by but not visible as Jase and Geneva submerged.

We're here! We want to take you someplace safe. Will you trust us? he asked, Geneva at his side. They were hand in hand, the insulation over their fingers only slightly dampening her connection to the sirenians.

And the sea cows did appear—all four metric tons of them. Jase was taken aback by their size. Their length was three times that of the nine-foot-long Florida manatees, but they were just as graceful in the water.

He felt Geneva squeeze his hand and point with her free one. Across the male sea cow's back was a huge harpoon scar. Jase's blood turned as icy as the waters as he studied the size and depth of the old injury. But that cold feeling left as he concentrated on the female. She was of reproductive age, as was the male. And if he wasn't sadly mistaken, she was pregnant!

Come with me, mother, he urged. *We have a safe haven waiting for you and your baby.*

The female hesitated, then came close enough for Jase to touch her. Next came the difficult part—convincing her to swim into the net that the crane had lowered in the water. The Steller's sea cows were cognizant of the lethal properties of nets and were terrified. To Jase's surprise, it was Geneva who was able to convince the female to submit to the net. It was Geneva who rode in the net with her through the nerve-racking journey through the air, over the deck and down into the cargo bay's Plexiglas tanks.

"Stay in the cargo bay with the female and keep her calm!" Jase called out to her from the choppy surface of the water. "She's pregnant!"

"I know!" Geneva gave him a thumbs-up signal and a big, wide grin.

Jase merely breathed a sigh of relief. Geneva had been in the water long enough. If he was already feeling the cold, he knew she must be, too, although he certainly wouldn't have guessed it by the large smile on her face. Jase allowed himself one last lingering thought of Geneva, then set himself to complete the task at hand.

The male sea cow was more difficult to net. He was reluctant to leave his feeding grounds, and frantic when his sonar couldn't locate his mate. To make matters worse, Jase discovered that the male's memory had irrevocably connected the harpoon scar and resulting pain with nets.

I know this net frightens you, but you're safe. There are no harpoons here! We won't hurt you!

The male remained unconvinced, despite Jase using

every ounce of his willpower. He finally had to send one of his crew to retrieve Geneva.

"Jase, what's wrong?" she called down to him, holding tightly the ship's rail in the choppy seas.

"Change of plan! I can't get the male into the net. I need you to do it!" Even from his lower position in the water, Jase could see Geneva's surprise.

"Me, Jase?"

"Yes, you! You have more power over the sea cows than I do! Your work with the female proved that! If you can stand the cold, I need you back in the water!" His breath left puffs of white in the cold arctic air.

"I'm on my way," Geneva yelled back. Still suited, she hurried over to the diving platform to quickly rejoin him.

Jase watched in awe as Geneva held his hand and then made mental contact with the male. She was immediately able to convince the cow to swim into the net with her and Jase. There was a tense moment when the net lifted and he started thrashing about, but again Geneva was able to calm him. It was Jase, not the confident Geneva, who anxiously held his breath before the male was finally deposited in the cargo holding tank. And it was Jase who hugged Geneva with relief, instead of the other way around.

"He had me worried," Jase said as he helped her out of the net and onto the deck. "You were great, Geneva!"

"Well, I don't know about that," she said with a shaky sigh. "But thank goodness we got the job done."

"And none too soon," Jase added. They both fought against the heavy pitching of the *Star of the Sea* as they headed toward the cow's holding tanks and the diving lockers. "We're in for one hell of a storm. I've already ordered the crew to head south."

For The Sanctuary...

"I'm sure your ship will be fine. But what about the sea cows?" Geneva asked as they hurried below deck, away from the frigid salt spray. "Are they all right?" She turned toward their prizes, her eyes intent on them as the crew helped strip them of their tanks and gear, leaving only the dry suits for them to remove on their own.

"The male's a bit agitated, but I think so. See for yourself," Jase said, holding out a hand to her. Geneva took it and concentrated. She smiled as her mind merged with the sea cows'.

"Sure beats getting in the tank with them and doing a medical exam," she managed to get out, her teeth chattering.

Jase frowned, his exhilaration over a successful capture fading beside his concern for Geneva. He took the blankets and terry-cloth robes one crew member held, set them on a dry section of the deck, then motioned for everyone to leave.

"Strip, Geneva."

Geneva tilted her head at him with amazement. "Isn't this where we came in?"

"What?" He peeled open the zipper flap and unzipped her suit. "Oh, at the pier..." he said with sudden understanding.

"With my Florida manatees." She smiled. "You've gotta come up with a better line, Jase," she said, clumsily trying to help him pull off her dry suit.

"Geneva, your hands are like ice! Let's get you changed and back to my cabin. I should never have let you back in the water!" He peeled off the top half, then lowered her to the pile of blankets. His words were rough, but his hands were infinitely gentle as he pulled off the lower half of the suit and insulated boots, then started on the nylon jumpsuit.

"Hey, I'm the sirenian expert," she said happily. "You never would have got my sea cows in the net without me."

"Probably not," Jase admitted as he discarded her nylon shell. He stared with dismay at her white, shivering limbs as he helped her with a robe, then stripped out of his own dry suit and put on another robe. He retrieved two pairs of regular arctic boots so he and Geneva would have something to wear on their way back to the cabin. Finally, he sat down next to her again and wrapped a blanket around her shoulders.

Geneva's hand immediately emerged to curl around his wrist. She watched the sea cows in the Plexiglas tank that took up most of the cargo hold, then turned toward Jase.

"You know," she said slowly, "I don't think I ever really, truly believed you could talk to animals until today."

Jase grinned. "So, my female Dr. Doolittle, how's it feel?"

"It's a pretty neat trick."

"It's no trick," Jase replied. He watched as she put on her boots, then turned toward the sea cows. "It's a Sanctuary power."

"Whatever it is, Jase, it's incredible."

"As are you." Jase put on his own boots, not bothering to zip them up in his hurry to retrieve two parkas from the storage lockers. "I couldn't have done it without you."

"We make a good team." She continued to watch

the cows, their massive bodies quiet in repose at the bottom of the tank. "Did you see that harpoon scar on the male?" she asked quietly.

Jase nodded. "It must have been pretty bad at the time."

"Yes. I'm so glad I was here to help."

"I'm glad we were *both* here." Jase pulled her to her feet and draped the parka around her shoulders. "It's not often I meet my equal, Geneva."

"Are we equals, Jase?"

"Yes. I know that as surely as I know the ocean's tides." *She was his only soulmate. There would never be another.*

Geneva leaned her cheek against his chest. "How much longer do we have, Jase?"

Jase couldn't bring himself to answer. The mood in the cargo bay suddenly changed, the tension as thick as the salt spray above deck.

Geneva lifted her head, her voice troubled. "The two weeks until we reach the barriers?"

"Not even that." Jase looked her straight in the eye. "You won't be going back to The Sanctuary with me. You go home tomorrow."

Chapter Eleven

"Tomorrow?" The shock in her eyes mirrored the pain in her heart. "So soon?"

Jase forced himself to go on. "The Sanctuary honors its business deals promptly. Your brother is already here in Nome. You and Thomas will be flying back to Florida together."

"I thought—" Geneva's voice broke as she strove for control. "I thought we'd go back to The Sanctuary together! I could help get the sea cows settled, and you and I..."

Jase steeled his heart. "That was not part of our bargain. You have what you want, I have what I want. Our business is now concluded."

"Do we, Jase? Do we really have what we want?" The desperation in her voice tore at his soul.

"No," he said harshly. He reached for her face and cupped her pale, lovely cheeks in his palms. "But we'll still have tonight, Sweet Survivor. If nothing else, we will have that."

Geneva closed her eyes. Jase watched as her soft breaths made little steam puffs in the cargo hold's chilled air. When Geneva opened her eyes again, the expression on her face was filled with sadness. "That's not much time, Jase."

"No." Desperate hunger gripped Jase's heart. "But it's all we have."

"Then…" Geneva's eyes lifted to his in a silent question, a question Jase immediately recognized.

"Not here, Geneva. Not here."

He refused to make love to her in a cold, unheated cargo hold. He refused to share her company with the sea cows. He wanted her alone in his cabin where he could lock the door and have her all to himself. Where he could turn up the heat, turn down the lights, strip her beautifully, gloriously naked, and revel in every inch of her.

Inside and out…

The well-trained crew didn't blink an eye or turn a head as Jase led her into his cabin and locked the door.

The instant they were in the room Geneva threw her parka on the floor and threw herself at him. Her kisses were frantic, her motions insistent, but Jase would have none of it. He firmly set her down on the bed in a jumble of parka, terry cloth, blankets and boots and pulled away.

"Stay still, Geneva!" he ordered when she rose on her knees to reach for him again. "Don't move!" He didn't want some quick, frantic coupling that would be over before they knew it. He wanted to stretch out this moment, enjoy the anticipation and relish every second.

"I want to move!" Geneva said, echoing her earlier words on a hot, tropical beach. "I want to make you move—*now*. Get undressed."

Those words alone sent blood coursing through his body in heated throbs. "Not yet."

"Not yet?" To his delight, her voice rose in frustration. "Why?"

"I want to enjoy this. I want us to savor this."

Geneva deliberately reached for his robe to pull him down on the bed with her. Jase allowed it, but he only sat. He wouldn't lie next to her, nor would he let her remove his robe. When Geneva insisted, he grabbed both her wrists and held them carefully with one hand.

"Slowly, Geneva," he whispered as he lowered her kneeling body to a seated position on his bed. "Slowly."

When she no longer tried to clutch at him, he released her. His hands reached for the towel around her head and began to dry her wet hair, for the dry suits tended to leak at the facial openings.

"Jase, for heaven's sake! My hair's full of seawater! There's no sense drying it when I'll just have to wash it in a little bit," Geneva said irritably.

"We're going to be here more than a little bit," he murmured. Geneva inhaled sharply; his meaning was quite clear. He took his time, stopping only once to go get a fresh, dry towel and his brush. He ran the bristles through her ebony tresses with slow, sensuous strokes. By the time her hair was damp-dry and brushed thoroughly, Geneva was trembling under his hands.

"You have a gentle touch," she said, watching him put the brush away and hang up the used towels.

"I used to work with children," he revealed. "It brought out the best in me." He removed her arctic boots, then his own and rejoined her on the bed.

"Children?" Geneva said hesitantly.

"It was a long time ago." His eyes caressed her body as his hand slowly covered and caressed her abdomen. "You'd bear such beautiful children, Geneva. If only we could…"

He didn't allow himself to complete that thought. Instead, he removed the blanket from her shoulders and folded first it, then his own. Then, his gaze never leaving her, he stowed them both away.

"This is taking forever," Geneva murmured, but Jase heard no irritation this time. He heard breathless anticipation—the same anticipation he was feeling and had wanted her to feel.

Jase made certain his own robe was securely belted before reaching for the ties of hers. His own arousal was outlined beneath the white terry cloth, but Geneva's was just as evident in her flushed cheeks and shallow breathing. He stood over her and untied her belt. Slowly, ever so slowly, he pushed the robe off her and down her arms, leaving it puddled at her waist.

He sat down close beside her, committing to memory her face, her shoulders, her breasts. Under his gaze her nipples tightened and darkened. Geneva leaned toward him as his hands lifted again, but he didn't reach for her breasts as she'd wanted. He pushed her back gently upon the pillows, instead.

Geneva moaned softly in frustration and reached for the robe at her waist to toss it aside.

"Don't, Geneva. I want to do that."

Slowly Geneva's hands released the terry cloth. But she had her revenge. She placed both hands behind her head, the motion proudly lifting her breasts, as she knew it would. The sight forced Jase to take in a deep breath before removing the rest of the robe from her body.

"If you don't hurry…" Geneva half warned, half

pleaded, her voice urgent in his ears as Jase deliberately turned away to hang up her robe.

He sat down on the bed for the last time. "My God, but you're beautiful," he whispered. "If I touch you, could you possibly stay still for me?"

Geneva shook her head, the ebony hair spreading out across the pillows. "Can't we...?"

"Soon," he whispered. "I want to know your body like my own."

The pupils in Geneva's eyes were huge. But she allowed him his request. "Can I touch you back?"

"Soon," he repeated. Jase lightly brushed his lips against hers. Then, with his hands, he traced the delicate ridge of her collarbone and traveled down the outside of her arms to her hands. He kissed every one of her fingers, then lingered on her palms. Finally he placed her hands back at her sides, brushed another light kiss on her mouth and continued with his slow, leisurely explorations. Not an inch of her exposed body missed his attentions, nor did his lips miss kissing any of those areas he'd attended to. First he touched, then he kissed, over and over again, back and forth, lower and lower.

By the time his lips were anointing the last of her ten toes, the bed sheets were tightly clutched between Geneva's fingers. Her thighs were open, her back was arched, her neck was extended back into the pillows. Jase knew she was ready. More than ready. But he waited. Even though his anticipation was now more painful than pleasurable, his wish to prolong the moment was greater still.

"Aren't you going to get undressed?" Geneva gasped as he covered her with his clothed body, his robe brushing sweetly against her sensitized breasts as he kissed the corner of one brown eye.

And suddenly Jase couldn't wait any longer. He sat up and threw the robe to the cabin floor, leaving it there. Jase quickly, eagerly covered her naked body with his own.

"Tell me what you want, Geneva."

He held off complete possession of her while waiting for her response. He felt her hands stroke the hair at the back of his neck.

"I didn't want this. This isn't how I imagined saying goodbye," Geneva said in a quiet voice. "I thought we'd be together under a hot sun and on warm sand instead of..."

She gestured toward the cabin porthole. Just outside was the darkness of an arctic night, a frigid, inhospitable ocean, and land covered with ice and snow. Inside were the trappings of civilized man, from the high-tech captain's intercom system to the synthetic sheets on the bed.

"We're together, Geneva. That, not the actual place, is what matters." He moved and aligned himself over her. "Tell me how to love you. Tell me what you want."

Her eyes were bright with unshed tears. Geneva shook her head, unable to answer. Instead she pulled him even closer, desperately urging him onward until they were united in the most intimate of embraces, the icy cold of the arctic disappearing in the warmth of the two of them together.

Then his passion met her fierceness, surpassed it and refused to leave her behind. They were equal partners, first one leading, the the other. Sometimes they jockeyed for dominance, but the struggle only added to the pleasure.

It wasn't until he silently brought first her, then himself, to exquisite, shuddering release that she finally spoke again and answered his question of earlier.

"What I want—what I really want," Geneva whispered in a broken voice, "is for this to last forever."

And Jase, physically satisfied but emotionally drained, finally realized how bittersweet life could be.

GENEVA WOKE HERSELF UP when she tried to roll over toward Jase and found nothing but a crumpled pillow.

"Better stop before you end up on the floor," Jase warned from across the room.

Geneva blinked. It was morning, and she was perched precariously on the free side of the narrow ship's bunk.

She looked up at him. Her spirits faded as she saw that Jase was dressed, and sunlight was flooding the cabin. "What time is it?"

"Time for you to go."

Those brutal words shook Geneva to the core and forced blunt honesty from her. "Jase, please come back to Florida with me. We could be happy, I know it."

Jase shook his head. "I wouldn't be any happier in your world than you'd be in mine. At least in The Sanctuary I have my work. It's not the sun and the moon and the stars, but it's something worthwhile. Something to get me up in the morning. I need that."

Geneva started to beg, to plead, but the resolute set to his jaw put an end to that. "Will we see each other again?" she forced herself to ask.

He averted his head and didn't answer. But Geneva saw the tremor pass through his body, and knew.

Again she forced some small modicum of dignity upon herself, for his sake as much as for hers.

"Will you at least tell me your real name?"

"Jason is my real name."

Geneva hugged the knowledge to herself. "I'd like to know the rest of it."

"No." The refusal was softly but firmly given. "That man died a long time ago, Geneva. I'm Jase Guardian of The Sanctuary. That's who I am now. And that's where I remain."

Geneva felt her heart contract, and she closed her eyes with pain. They opened again as she felt him sit beside her on the bed, his arms offering consolation that couldn't cure the raw agony deep inside. She reached for him with desperate, almost frenzied movements.

"Again, Jase. Make love to me one last time."

He kissed her tenderly on the forehead, and shook his head. "I'm sorry, Geneva."

"Jase, please!" she cried as he stood up. "Stay with me!"

"I can't." He lifted his parka in one hand and headed for the cabin door. "I won't."

She grabbed the sheet and sprang out of the narrow bunk, unwilling to let him go. "Why not?"

"Because... Because it would break my heart."

There was such truth, such anguish in his words that Geneva's own heart shattered into tiny pieces. When he left for the bridge, he didn't slow down as he exited through the cabin door. He didn't even turn around.

Nor did she call him back.

THE TWO-WEEK SAIL from Alaska to the warm Caribbean waters was over. Jase's smaller boat from The

Sanctuary was waiting outside of the barriers. The crew loaded his things aboard, then assisted as Jase off-loaded the sea cows into the ocean. The sirenians cooperated fully, and soon the *The Star of the Sea* was sailing off into the distance.

Jase Guardian was alone....

He watched as his delphine wards arrived through the barriers and cavorted playfully around the boat. For once he couldn't share in the joy of their reunion. His thoughts were only on Geneva and how desperately he missed her. The presence of her sea cows only served to underscore his loneliness. Geneva and Thomas were already back in Florida and had been for some time. Jase had deliberately kept tabs on her. His contacts had told him she'd taken a leave of absence from work. She and Thomas were staying in Miami with the aunt and uncle who had raised Geneva, and they had flown there from Alaska instead of to Geneva's home town in Jacksonville.

As for Jase, he'd soon return to his old life in The Sanctuary.

And that would be the end.

It had been hard, but he'd finally done it. Jase had let Geneva go. He prayed Thomas would be able to help her through the rough times she had ahead. If their separation was tearing at her at even a fraction of the amount it was him, she'd need her twin's support. That applied not only to her personal life but to her professional one as well, for Geneva had announced to the world that she'd been unable to relocate the sea cows.

Jase only hoped she'd suffer no serious retribution at the Sirenian Institute. He prayed she wouldn't suffer at all, but he remembered her bowed head as she'd been put ashore, remembered her final farewell wave and knew his hope was in vain.

They were *both* in pain.

Jase started the boat engines with a savage twist of the key and flipped the switch to raise the anchor. Slowly, so as to allow the sea cows to easily keep pace, Jase headed for the barriers.

He recalled Geneva's final words while she had waited for the small water taxi that would take her in to shore.

"Thanks for everything, Jase. Too bad I have to change from Dr. Doolittle back to plain old Dr. Kelsey again." She'd actually managed a smile. "Still, I'm glad I had a chance to talk to them, even if it was only for a little while. Take good care of my sea cows. And yourself. I love you, Jase."

Jase thought of a million replies, a million things he wanted to say. Like how he felt toward her. How he'd miss her. How grateful he was for her love. How he'd lay the wealth of the ocean at her feet if he could. Instead he'd reached for her and held her tightly, his face buried in her hair, the words staying locked inside him.

Jase cursed himself. He should have said *something*. Like *I love you, too, Geneva*. Instead, he'd silently let her leave his life. Jase shook his head, then made a slight course adjustment at the ship's wheel. He'd allowed his attention to wander, and that wasn't a smart thing to do in the barriers. The skies grew blacker, the water darker. Jase's keen eyesight could barely make out the dolphins now, and the sea cows not at all, although he sensed their presence close by.

The nails of both hands dug into the rounded wood

beneath Jase's palms. He hated accepting that he'd never see Geneva Kelsey again, yet knew the odds were hopeless once he crossed back into The Sanctuary. He didn't want to cross over. He wanted to slow the boat—no, *stop* the boat and turn around. *He wanted Geneva back.*

But that could never be. So, with teeth clenched and heart aching, Jase Guardian passed through the barriers.

"I'M SORRY, GENEVA. I really tried to pass that test, but…" Thomas's disappointment, and Geneva's, lay thick in the air.

"It's okay, Thomas. Maybe it's just as well." Geneva sighed. "You're a little old to be worrying about high school, anyway. Maybe we should look into finding a tutor, instead."

"Why bother?" Thomas rose from the wicker patio chair. He paced back and forth on his aunt's front porch overlooking the ocean. "You and I both know it's hopeless. I don't know how to drive. I don't know how to use a computer, or your bank's automated teller or a VCR. Hell, I didn't even know what a VCR was! So why the surprise that I can't pass a high school equivalency exam?"

"You had a perfect score on the biology portion of the test," Geneva said, trying to force a note of encouragement into her voice.

"That's about all anyone learns in The Sanctuary. That, and oceanography. My Sanctuary knowledge sure isn't going to get me a job here in Florida," he said with disgust.

"Shh!" Geneva looked in the front window where

their elderly aunt was inside watching her favorite afternoon TV soap opera. "She'll hear you."

"That's another thing I hate," Thomas complained. "I can't talk to *anyone* about *anything!* The last twenty years of my life are off limits. I had friends—special friends."

Thomas's voice broke off, and suddenly Geneva remembered the young woman she'd seen in Thomas's quarters.

"But now I have to pretend I was Robinson Crusoe shipwrecked alone for twenty years."

"I know it's hard."

"It's more than hard, it's terrible! I hate lying to everyone, Geneva! Sooner or later I'm going to trip up, and then what?"

"It'll be better once we move back to my place," Geneva assured him. "Miami's a huge city. Jacksonville is much slower paced, and we'll be away from all Dad's Miami relatives."

"I don't *want* to move away from Miami! At least here I'm on the beach."

"Well, Jacksonville is on a river. The St. Johns, remember?"

"That's not the same as being near the ocean! And even if it was, I don't intend to mooch off my sister the rest of my life! Damn it, Geneva, I don't have much. At least let me hold on to my pride."

Geneva shifted uneasily in her seat. "You'll find a job, Thomas. It'll just take some time."

"With no education? I'm thirty-five years old! I can't even pass a high school entrance exam! And that's not the half of it. I have no paperwork, no records...I don't even have a social security number or a driver's license! Who the hell is going to hire me? The only job I'm qualified for is that of Sanctuary guard—''

"Don't say it!" Geneva quickly interrupted. "Don't even think it! Maybe I could get you a job at the Sirenian Institute."

Thomas's smile wasn't pleasant. "As what? Men's room janitor? Not that they'd hire the brother of the woman who just 'lost' the find of the century."

Geneva winced. She'd taken a lot of flak from her superiors over the supposed "loss" of the sea cows. Much more than she'd let on...

"You may fool the family by telling everyone you're on vacation, but you can't fool me. My twin thing says you're in big trouble, Geneva. You may be out of a job yourself."

"It'll work out eventually," Geneva said miserably.

"Sure it will. And The Sanctuary's going public tomorrow."

Geneva bristled at her twin's sarcasm. "Well, what was I supposed to tell them? That I traded the cows for your release from the Bermuda Triangle?"

"Why not?" Thomas flung back at her. "At least it would be the truth. I'm tired of lying! I'm tired of you lying for me! I'm tired of feeling like a fish out of water!"

"Readjustment will take time."

Thomas glared at her. "And I'm *really* sick and tired of you telling me everything's going to be all right. It's not!"

"Thomas!" Geneva cried as her twin flung himself off the porch. "Where are you going?"

"To the beach for a swim!"

"You can't run to the beach every time a problem comes up!" Geneva yelled after him, not caring if her aunt heard her or not. "You have to stand up and face the facts!"

"I've faced them, Geneva!" Thomas whirled around on the boardwalk, his face stiff with frustration. "Why don't you?"

The words hit Geneva like a knife to the heart.

She *had* faced the cruel facts, and they weren't easy to live with. The naked truth of the matter burned like an unquenchable flame. *She wanted Jase back.* She thought she could walk away from him and had found herself desperately, horribly wrong. Now that she knew she couldn't live without him, no matter *where* he lived, it was too late.

Jase was gone. She couldn't find her way back into The Sanctuary any more than Thomas could.

"Thomas, please come back...."

He refused to slow down. Geneva hurried after him, but lost him on the beach amid the happy shouts of tourists and locals alike enjoying the Miami waves. Geneva sighed. It wasn't really her brother she wanted. She wanted Jase and the happiness that had eluded her ever since her departure from the *Star of the Sea.*

Fully clothed, she waded into the water, shoes and all. If she closed her eyes, she could almost pretend she was in Jase's lagoon again. The dolphins would play at her feet as Jase put his arms around her, then she'd hold him tight and never let him go....

Ever.

Geneva took another few steps out into the water, her eyes on the far horizon. The warm ocean moved up over the hems of her shorts, but Geneva felt as icy as the Alaskan waters where she had bid Jase goodbye.

"Hey, lady, are you okay?" someone shouted.

I'm not okay. I may never be okay again, came the bleak thought.

"Lady, why don't you come out of the water?"

From out of the corner of her eye, Geneva saw a red cross on a white T-shirt: the lifeguard's insignia. She refused to take her gaze off the horizon, however. Somewhere out there was The Sanctuary—and the man she loved.

"I'll take care of her," another voice said. "She's family."

"Get her home, okay?" ordered the lifeguard. "She's making me very nervous."

"I will."

Geneva felt Thomas's hands on her shoulders. Still she refused to turn away from the distant horizon.

"Where the hell *is* our home, Geneva?"

"I think you know the answer to that, Thomas," Geneva said softly. "At least for you, anyway."

"What about you, Geneva? What about family? And your job? Florida may not be home to me, but I know it is to you."

"It was. Maybe it still is. I don't know. All I know is that I can't live without Jase. I thought I could, but I can't." She felt her heart wrench with loss. "I have to be with him, Thomas. I want to go back."

"So do I, but we can't! You don't know how to get back, Geneva! *I* don't know how to get back!"

She felt Thomas's hands tighten with frustration on her shoulders. Finally Geneva turned toward her twin. The anguish in his face mirrored her own. "We have to try."

"How?"

"First we'll find out who Jase Guardian really is. I think I know a way to identify him."

"And then?" Thomas's eyes shone with desperate hope.

"Once I know who he is, we'll find out *where* he is. And then we'll go back. *Both* of us."

"JASE, YOU JUST RETURNED!" the Senior Guardian argued. "I cannot permit another absence! I cannot spare you so soon!"

For once, Jase refused to be swayed by the older man's wishes. "I want to go back to the mainland," he insisted.

"You mean you want to go back to Geneva Kelsey," the Senior Guardian corrected him. "You've pined for her since your return to The Sanctuary."

"I won't deny that I miss her. But I want to leave to see my brother. I didn't have a chance to visit with him this time. I always see Shawn when I go to the mainland. You know that."

Jase saw the Senior Guardian hesitate and pressed his advantage. "I was unable to do so because of the sea cows. Now that they're safely situated here, I want to go back to Miami to see Shawn."

Jase watched as the Senior Guardian considered his words.

"Just Shawn?"

Jase gave the other man a cynical smile. "Surely you don't think Geneva Kelsey is going to show up at Shawn's private institution, do you? It's not as if she knows who or where he is."

"No, I suppose not." There was a pause, then the older man said, "I will watch your wards. But only for a very short time. Do not make me come after you. Your work is here, Jase Guardian."

The warning was very clear, Jase realized as he

watched the Senior Guardian head for the path leading to the lagoon. Well, that was too damn bad.

"Jason Merrick has unfinished business elsewhere," he said aloud, his eyes on the retreating figure. "And Shawn isn't even the half of it."

"THIS MUST BE the hundredth bookstore we've tried," Thomas groaned as Geneva parked the car at yet another shopping mall. "If you take me into one more shopping center I'll go crazy."

Geneva reached for her twin's hand. After twenty years of living mostly outside, Thomas had proved to be slightly claustrophobic amid crowds of people, especially while indoors.

"I know, Thomas, but we have to keep looking. The library where I did my initial research on the Bermuda Triangle didn't have an up-to-date list of the missing ships. I remember telling myself I was going to order the most recent publication on the subject, but then Jase showed up, and—"

Geneva abruptly broke off. She missed him so much, it hurt.

"He swept you off your feet." Thomas gave her an understanding kiss on the cheek, then climbed out of the car, limping all the while in his new sneakers. "Well, let's get this over with before my own feet give out," he said as he opened Geneva's car door. "I'd give anything to feel Sanctuary sands right now."

"You will, Thomas. As soon as we find a book that lists the last five years of missing ships." Geneva frowned. "Unfortunately, Bermuda Triangle books aren't exactly bestsellers."

Three bookstores and a few blisters later, they struck pay dirt.

"Geneva!" Thomas yelled from his spot at the discounted sale bin. "I've found one!" He flipped through the table of contents, but Geneva ripped the book from her twin with uncharacteristic impatience.

"Let me," she said as she found the page number and turned toward it with fingers trembling from excitement. "Here we are. This is current all the way through last September!"

Under "marine casualties," she scanned back five years, then read line by line, with Thomas peering over her shoulder.

"He said his real name was Jason. Look for Jase or Jason." Suddenly she gasped.

"What?"

Geneva pointed to the stark black letters contained in one year's column of statistics.

Merrick, Jason. Presumed lost at sea: December 19.

Geneva's marine biologist's brain kicked into overdrive. Dolphins! Dr. Jason Merrick had worked with dolphins and autistic children! He was the one who'd used the phrase *common denominator* that had stuck in her mind.

"Geneva?" Thomas pressed, but Geneva was busy remembering how Dr. Merrick's lab had been destroyed. She recalled how his dolphins had been killed, along with his therapist: the same therapist who the newspapers had said was Jase's lover. Jase had been unsuccessfully sued for criminal negligence by the woman's parents. And Jase's autistic brother had inherited everything from the Merrick estate except a cure.

Anyone, even a layman, let alone a marine biologist, would remember that sensational trial. It was in the media for weeks!

Oh, Jase, no wonder you left this world behind, Geneva silently cried. *There was nothing left in it for you! Nothing at all...except for me. And weighed against everything else, I never had a chance.*

The book slipped from her hands and dropped to the floor, much to the counter clerk's dismay. Thomas ignored the fallen book and crumpled pages, his whole attention on his twin's shaking body.

"You know who he is now?"

"Yes." Geneva lifted a desperate, white face to her brother. "I have to find him, Thomas. I have to find him!"

"We will."

"Dear God, I hope so, Thomas. Because now I know..."

"What, Geneva?"

"He's never coming back."

Chapter Twelve

Jase felt the past rise up again as the limo drove through the expensive brick-and-wrought-iron fence gate and continued on through the carefully landscaped grounds before stopping. He stepped out of the car and started toward the double glass doors, knowing the driver would wait without having to give the order.

The sanitarium doors hissed open as Jase stepped inside the electronic beam. He walked straight to the front counter and the bored male attendant doing a crossword puzzle to the tune of a top-forty radio station.

"I'm here to see Shawn Merrick," Jase announced.

The attendant rolled his eyes upward at being distracted, although he did take his feet off the top of his desk. "Your name?"

"Merrick."

The attendant yawned without bothering to cover his mouth. "Which Merrick? Tom, Dick or Harry?"

"Jason Merrick. I'm his brother."

"Quit yanking my chain, buddy. Shawn's got no brother, and I'm busy." The man went back to his puzzle.

Jase reached over the counter, grabbed the man's

shirt and effortlessly lifted him to his feet. The cross-word book fell to the floor.

"I'd like his room number, please." Jase continued to keep a tight hold on the man's shirt. *God help Shawn if these were the kind of people caring for him,* he thought angrily.

The male attendant took one look at Jase's eyes, nervously reached for his computer with one hand and quickly tapped in Shawn's name. "Room 214."

Jase carefully lowered the man back into his chair again, then released his shirt. "Thank you."

"You're welcome, sir." Jase noticed that the attendant now reached for a pile of charts instead of his crossword puzzle book. "Left at the end of the hall, first room on the right."

Jase crossed the lobby and headed for the room with measured steps. How long had it been since he'd been in this place? Worse yet, how long had Shawn been in this place?

The first question was easier to answer than the last. *Ever since his records were destroyed in the bomb explosion.*

That was when Jason Merrick had discarded everything in the real world for the safe confines of The Sanctuary. He'd held fast to that practice, discarding Geneva Kelsey in the process.

What a mistake he'd made! And how painfully he'd paid for that error! He wouldn't—*couldn't*—live without her. And the decision to acknowledge his love for Geneva meant he had no choice but to acknowledge the real world again.

The real world of Shawn Merrick. And Jason Merrick. And the work he'd given up so long ago.

He'd had too much time to think since he'd fool-

ishly sent Geneva away. During that time Dr. Jason
Merrick had reemerged; his rusty psychologist's mind-
set was again activated.

*If dolphins can talk to the autistic, and I can talk
to the dolphins, doesn't it logically follow that I can
talk to the autistic? That I can talk to Shawn?*

He had to find out if he was right. He had to find
out if one man, one person, could really make a difference. He'd discovered that he could in The Sanctuary. But could he make a difference in the real world
again? Could he put the past behind him and begin a
new life—with Geneva?

Geneva's love had given him the courage to begin
again. Jase refused to walk away from her challenge,
or her. Could he ever fit into the real world, in *her*
world, again?

He had to know.

His hand didn't waver as he first knocked, then
opened the door to Room 214. Shawn's personal attendant looked up from his paperback as Jase walked
in.

"Would you mind waiting outside?" Jase asked.

"Sure." The attendant stood.

Jase closed the door after the man had left the room.

Jase and Shawn were left alone.

"Hi, Shawn."

Jase joined his brother on the plush carpet of the
floor and studied him. Outwardly, Shawn was clean,
neat, trimmed and even passably shaved. But there the
normalcy ended. Shawn Merrick was a huddled ball
of thin, withdrawn humanity who sat rocking back and
forth, over and over again.

"It's me. Jase. It's been a long time, Shawn." He

reached out to touch his brother, knowing Shawn would recoil but wanting to touch him, anyway.

Contact was made. Shawn violently pushed away and continued his rocking, the motions more frenzied this time. Jase hid the pain of Shawn's rejection. After all these years, he could never get used to it.

"I met someone, Shawn," he said softly. "I think you'd like her. She's not here now, but maybe later you could meet her...."

Oh, God, this was ridiculous. He was stalling for time, delaying rather than facing disappointment again. He'd had so damn much disappointment in his life.

Well, best get it over with. He'd weathered setbacks before. He would weather them again. His future with Geneva was at stake. It was now or never.

Jase steeled himself and concentrated.

Hello, Shawn. It's your brother, Jase. Do you remember me?

"WE'RE HERE TO BUY A BOAT," Geneva announced to the salesman.

"That's right. And this is what we want." Thomas handed the man the sheet of paper listing the preferred specifications.

"Are we talking new or used?"

"New," Geneva stated. "And I'm not financing this. I'm paying cash."

The salesman immediately brightened up and glowed like a two-hundred-watt bulb. "One moment. Let me get my fliers for you. I'll be right back."

"Boat prices have sure gone up in the past twenty years! Geneva, are you sure you can afford this?" Thomas hissed as the salesman hurried off.

"Yep. I sold my car, sublet my apartment and tapped into my savings." Geneva strolled over to a promising looking vessel, Thomas at her side. "Money's the least of our problems. The problem's going to be finding the barriers."

"You know, Geneva, I've been thinking. And I've come to the conclusion that I might be able to—you know—feel them."

"Feel the barriers? Oh, Thomas, really?"

"I've lived within their confines for twenty years. Maybe I can hone in on them. But don't get your hopes up," Thomas warned as Geneva gave him a joyful hug. "Just because I *might* be able to find the barriers doesn't mean we can get through them. I don't know how, Sis. I didn't take the pledge, so I was never shown."

Geneva felt her hopes rise just the same. "We'll find a way, Thomas."

He gave her a rueful grin. "Or die trying…"

JASE HUNG UP the private phone in the limo with a muttered curse. His fourth phone call had gone no better than the previous ones. His lips tightened into a thin line as he recalled the conversations.

"I'm sorry, Mr. Guardian, but Geneva Kelsey's not here. I'm the new tenant. She's sublet her apartment…. No, I don't know where she is. My rent goes directly into her bank account."

His call to the Sirenian Institute was no more successful. "I'm sorry, but Dr. Kelsey is on an extended leave of absence. No, we don't know how to contact her. I'm afraid I can't help you…."

In desperation, he'd called up her aunt and uncle in Miami. "She and Thomas left here yesterday. I was under the impression they went back to Alaska for a reunion with relatives up there. After all, Thomas hasn't seen them for twenty years.... Yes, I have their numbers. Hold on..."

But the Alaskan relatives hadn't seen Geneva and Thomas Kelsey recently. Nor did they expect them.

The joy Jase had experienced after his visit to Shawn was long gone, replaced with sick, gut-churning worry. After speaking to Shawn the same way he spoke to his wards, the results had been so favorable that he immediately wanted to share them with Geneva.

He wanted to tell her how his brother had made eye contact...

How a flash of recognition had appeared in Shawn's face...

How, for the first time in years, Jase saw a human being before that violent rocking resumed....

Jase remembered the way his brother's mind had suddenly opened to him. It wasn't much, it wasn't even for very long. But it was a start, for both Shawn Merrick, and for Dr. Jason Merrick.

A start that had come to an abrupt halt. He was running out of time here in the real world. He should have returned to The Sanctuary long before now. It was only a matter of time before the Senior Guardian had others searching for him, others who would force him to go back.

Damn it, Geneva, where the hell are you?

And then suddenly, he knew. He didn't know how, but he *knew* that Geneva was out at sea. Looking for The Sanctuary. Looking for *him.* Jase's blood ran cold at the thought. For every trespasser who accidentally stumbled upon the way through the barriers, there were many more who didn't. The violent elements in the barriers could, and did, kill, despite The Sanctuary's efforts to preserve life. Every guardian knew that....

Jase rapped on the clear partition, then picked up the intercom phone.

"Get me to the marina. *Now*."

The driver nodded and picked up speed. Jase sat back again and replaced the phone with trembling hands. Despite the coolness of the limo's air-conditioning, he began to sweat.

"I NEVER COULD understand this place," Thomas yelled, the barriers' lightning illuminating the darkness of his face. He and Geneva held tightly to the ship's sway bars as the seas rocked their new craft with bone-jarring violence. "I'm telling you, I don't know how to get in!"

From the uncovered deck, Geneva stared at the fog-enshrouded phenomenon before them. After twelve nerve-racking hours, Thomas had indeed honed in on the barriers. But there his success ended.

"Try again, Thomas!" Geneva urged. "Three-fifths of this planet is ocean. Most of it is unexplored, but that doesn't mean its ways aren't comprehensible. The ocean here simply has its own laws of nature! It's up to us to make sense of them."

"Make sense of The Sanctuary?" Thomas asked with disbelief. "Twin, I'm lucky I even found this place again. *You're* the scientist. *You* explain how this place works!"

"Well, we'll just have to create a new scientific framework to explain the barriers." Geneva shivered within the dampness and pulled the neck of her waterproof jacket closer.

"A new framework?"

"Yes, an original point of reference. You can help. Try some free thinking! That's how Columbus discovered a new continent! That's how Pasteur discovered cures! That's how Einstein discovered relativity!"

Thomas turned away from her and looked out over the salt-sprayed deck into the darkness of the barriers. "I see fog that doesn't move correctly. I see lightning that has no sound. I see lights in the water that shouldn't be there." He shook his head in bewilderment. "I don't see anything that makes sense, Sis."

Geneva could have screamed with frustration. "Keep looking, Thomas! Even unpredictability can be predicted!"

"I don't know what I'm looking for! There's nothing out there but pure chaos."

"You have to see something!" Geneva insisted.

"I see rough seas and a gas tank half empty. Geneva, if we don't find the way through soon, we're going to have to turn back."

Geneva thought of Jase and tried to picture the rest of her life without him. That thought was infinitely more frightening than an empty gas tank. "I don't know about you, but I don't want to go back."

"Neither do I!" Thomas said vehemently. "But if we don't—"

Both twins felt the lurching of the craft beneath their feet. Geneva knew what he was going to say even before her twin said it.

"Without engine power in these seas, we're going down."

JASE OPENED THE THROTTLE wide, the engine and his heart both racing at full bore. He'd be at the barriers within thirty minutes. He'd been scanning the sea creatures' minds without success for some idea of Geneva's whereabouts. The fact that none of them—even his own personal wards—would help him was chilling. That meant they'd received orders from the Senior Guardian to remain silent. And that silence told him one thing.

Somehow, Geneva and Thomas had found their way back to the barriers.

"YOU'D BETTER PUT THIS ON." Thomas held out the life jacket to his twin, then grabbed another for himself. "We'll be losing engine power any time now. It'll be a real rough ride from there."

Geneva stared at the swells, which grew larger by the minute. Even with pointing the bow into the swell, any one of those monster waves could overturn their boat. If they were broadsided once they were out of fuel...

"I'm sorry, Geneva. I really did try." Thomas's voice was hoarse with emotion. "This isn't exactly what I had planned for our grand reunion."

"We're not giving up yet!" Geneva held tightly to the rail with both hands. She was soaked from the spray and shivering. "Jase will help us. I know he will."

"He doesn't even know where we are!"

Thomas's sentence was cut off as another huge wave swept over the deck. Geneva's knees buckled under the crushing weight of the water pouring down. She emerged coughing as Thomas realigned the boat into the direction of the swells.

Despite the waves, Geneva's mind remained only on Jase. Suddenly she remembered his words.

The Sanctuary gives its gifts only to those with predisposed abilities, Geneva. Because of all your work with them, you were already predisposed to sea cows. If you hadn't been predisposed, I would never have been able to help you hear them. Of course, since we're not in The Sanctuary, your powers are restricted.

But she was in The Sanctuary now!

"Thomas, I think I know how to find him!" Geneva said excitedly.

"Then do it, Sis. Because we just ran out of gas."

JASE HAD COVERED almost half of the barriers' circumference when he felt the female Steller's sea cow call for him. The contact took him totally by surprise.

The message is from a female? The female who is my mate? Jase immediately demanded and received confirmation, the message bringing renewed hope to his heart.

He immediately plotted a new course to the northeast reaches of the barriers and forced every ounce of speed he could from his craft.

"Hang on, Geneva. I'm coming!"

GENEVA CLUNG for dear life as the current pulled them farther into the destructive barrier waves with their fog and blue-green lights. So far their boat had escaped being totally swamped, but Geneva knew it was only a matter of time before the inevitable took place.

"Did you get through to the sea cows?" Thomas asked, once again wrestling with the controls. Engine power had died long ago, but the boat's rudder still sluggishly responded manually. "Did they actually hear you?"

"Yes! I'm predisposed, and this *is* The Sanctuary! They heard me!"

Another wave washed over them. The deck pitched horribly forward. Just when Geneva thought they would roll over, the boat righted itself. Both twins immediately made visual checks for each other.

"I'm all right!" Geneva reassured a frantic Thomas. "You keep your hands on the wheel!"

Thomas did just that, and Geneva blessed both his Sanctuary strength and his powers that enabled her twin to read the seas so well. She knew she would have lost control of the craft long ago.

"Do you think the sea cows gave Jase the message yet?" he shouted. "Ask them!"

Geneva concentrated, straining to receive the faintest of replies. Hope spread warm tendrils through her freezing body.

"He's coming, Thomas! He's coming!"

"I'M COMING, GENEVA!" *Tell her I'm coming!* Jase ordered the sea cows. *I'm almost there!*

Jase could have screamed from frustration as he tried to coax even more speed from his boat, and failed. He could go no faster. The barrier was violently making its presence known; its walls rising higher and higher with unforgiving ferocity. But at last he was able to make out the hazy form of Geneva and her twin on the deck of their craft.

She immediately turned toward him, her very posture crying for his help. Jase tried to project both mental and physical reassurance, but deep inside he felt neither. The other boat was pitching horribly and was dangerously close to capsizing. His own craft was almost as bad. Jase had never known the seas to be so harsh and cruel in the presence of a guardian. Even his wards had deserted him when confronted by the uncharacteristic fury of these Sanctuary seas.

His concentration on Geneva wavered when his keen sight picked up a tall-masted schooner in the far distance. It was quickly bearing down toward them. He saw Geneva's gaze, then Thomas's, follow his.

Nothing needed to be said. All three of them knew who that schooner belonged to and why he was here. And suddenly the Senior Guardian's wards relayed to him what was to be.

Jase would return to The Sanctuary. Geneva and Thomas would not be allowed back in.

"No!" Jase screamed his fury.

"Jase?" Geneva responded at his cry. "Jase?"

Jase couldn't hear Geneva, but he saw her mouth his name, saw the fear on her face. He felt for the sea cows and had them relay the horrible message to her.

The deal had been their freedom for the sea cows, and The Sanctuary always honored its deals. The Senior Guardian was here to ensure that the deal was rigidly adhered to. Jase saw despair color Geneva's face as the Senior Guardian's message was given. Then he gave her one of his own.

Tell my mate not to give up yet! he ordered the sea cows. *We will be together!*

Some of the tension eased on her face as Jase's craft approached from the east; the schooner approached Geneva's boat from the west. Then the three boats were within shouting distance of one another, their outlines and humans illuminated by the barrier's noiseless lightning. Jase's gaze locked with Geneva's. Despite the danger to her boat, she gave him a smile that spoke of total trust. Her life was in his hands, and they both knew it.

The Senior Guardian spoke first. "You are disobeying our rules, Jase. These two are no longer allowed here."

Jase ignored his superior. "Geneva, are you all right?" he yelled across the water.

Geneva nodded, even as Thomas shouted, "She's fine, Jase! But we're out of gas! I can't keep us afloat much longer!"

"You'll have to come aboard my vessel! I'll get closer and throw you a line."

"Jase, I forbid it!" the Senior Guardian ordered. "Hold your position!"

"No. I won't let them drown!"

"I will give them fuel and send them back to Miami, where they belong. And you will go back to The Sanctuary, Jase. Where *you* belong!"

"Geneva comes with me!" And Jase deliberately headed toward the Kelseys' craft.

"I told you he'd come!" Geneva threw Thomas a triumphant look. "I told you!"

"He won't get far, Sis. Look." Thomas pointed toward the roiling, churning water.

Visible now was a new barrier between her and Jase.

"Whales!" Geneva gasped.

"Yeah. A whole damn pod of them." Her twin slammed his fist on the metal dash above the controls. "They're right in front of us! Jase can't get through!"

Thomas swore a vicious, violent expletive. "Tell them to move, Senior Guardian!" he yelled out. "I want to take the pledge! And Geneva wants to be with Jase!"

"That is not possible," yelled the white-clothed figure of the Senior Guardian. "Jase alone stays. You two will never enter again."

Jase looked toward Geneva, then at the huge blue whales, their massive bodies easily seen, even in the fog. His eyes met hers with such anguish that she almost turned away, unable to face such naked pain.

Jase couldn't make them move. She could see it in his face, feel it in her heart as the whales closed ranks between her and the man she loved. The Senior Guardian looked down at the three of them from the lofty heights of the much-larger schooner, but still Jase refused to back down.

"Let her come to me!" Jase demanded.

"I shall not."

"You *will!*"

"Sanctuary business with the Kelseys is concluded."

"These are people, not business!" Jase's fury was so terrible that Geneva was frightened, even though his rage was not directed at her. "I need her! Either she stays, or I go! But either way, we remain together!"

"Geneva goes home without you. My wishes overrule yours, Jase. They always have."

"Not this time!" Jase cried with an intensity that shook Geneva to the core. She saw him glare furiously at the pod of whales. "Move your wards!"

"I refuse!"

"You *will!*" Jase screamed. *"You'll do it now!"*

"*I* am Senior here, Jase Guardian, not you. I will not move them. That is final."

Jase writhed inside, raging against his terrible feeling of helplessness. It reminded him how helpless he'd felt when Nanci died. And made him remember the dolphins who'd died under his protection. His hopes for Shawn had also fallen victim; they'd died with the destruction of his work. Those deaths had cost him dearly. And now he watched, helpless again, as another loved one was being taken from him.

With dead certainty, Jase knew that without Geneva, his own life would be forfeit. His survival depended on hers, and Geneva Kelsey was somehow, someway, miraculously here.

He wasn't ever letting her get away from him again.

Jase straightened even more, his eyes locked with the Senior Guardian's. Something deep inside him shattered and broke free of its chains and was replaced by determination and resolve.

"If you won't move them," he vowed, *"then I will."* Drawing on every ounce of strength that Geneva's love had given him, Jase concentrated.

The past meant nothing. The future was everything. And the injustice of losing Geneva forever roused him like nothing had ever done before.

You will move!

Jase felt the whales' astonishment at the force of his command and heard the Senior Guardian's "No, Jase, remember the rules!" even as he saw naked fear mix with desperate hope on Geneva's face.

"To hell with the rules!" *You will move!* he screamed with every single bit of mental power he possessed.

All four humans saw the great bodies hesitate.

You will move! Now! Now! Now! Now! Now! Now! Now! Now! Now! Now! Now! Now!

The Senior Guardian stumbled on his deck at the force of Jase's command. Thomas Kelsey gasped in amazement at the sight in the water. And Geneva Kelsey's champion watched with love and fierce triumph as the massive whales slowly, gracefully, parted a path for him.

Jase allowed himself a brief glance at his old mentor, then deliberately turned to claim his prize.

Her hair streaming in the wind, Geneva waited at the railing, her lovely face one of ethereal beauty as Jase approached. Despite the tossing of the boat, she released her grip and stretched her arms, fingers wide, out toward him. Not a word was said as Jase motored toward her, his eyes never leaving her. Not a word was said as he took her aboard his craft and drew her straight into his own arms.

No words were needed. As the seas calmed and the barriers quieted around Jase's craft, as the whales protectively encircled their new master and his mate, everyone knew who was now the most powerful.

After a long, long while, Jase's head finally lifted again to face his old mentor. "I'm going back to my island. Get your ship out of my way."

The older man stared in shock as Jase snapped out the order.

"You'll move now, old man, or I'll order these whales to move you! Either way, I'm going through the barriers. And Geneva's coming with me."

"I—I will move." The schooner's captain trembled, looking terribly old, terribly defeated. "Yes, I shall move...*Senior Guardian.*"

Jase turned back to Thomas, still on Geneva's boat. It now floated gently on the rapidly calming sea. "Refuel from the schooner's stocks, then follow the whales in. Geneva and I will join you later."

"Yes, Senior Guardian," Thomas replied in his most formal voice. "I pledge my loyalty to The Sanctuary and to its ruler."

Jase actually managed a smile. "Thomas, I'll be pledging you to the sharks if you don't give us some time alone," he said, cradling Geneva even closer while pressing a kiss on his beloved. "And I'd better not see you anywhere near my island when I get in, either."

"You don't have to draw me a picture." Thomas dropped his formal manner and gave Jase an answering grin. "Besides, I've got my own reunion to take care of. See you later, Sis."

Jase watched Geneva as she lifted her head to wave farewell. To his joy, her attention immediately returned to him. He basked in the love in her eyes while all the words and feelings he wanted to share with her warred for supremacy.

Like how foolish he'd been to let her go, and how he'd feared he'd never find her again.

How he'd wanted to tell her about his visit to Shawn.

And how he wanted to recreate his work with the autistic once more.

How shocked he'd been at her disappearance from Florida.

How overjoyed he was to find her with the help of the sea cows. And how very, very clever she was to call him through them.

How in the future he planned to have the ex-Senior Guardian be known as Elder Guardian and become Thomas's mentor.

And how he felt it was time for new rules for The Sanctuary. No one should ever have to go through the suffering he and Geneva had experienced.

And how he would make it all up to her, if she would just give him the chance.

But as Jase looked into her shining eyes, he decided to tell her the most important thing of all, the one thing he'd never, ever said.

"I love you, Geneva Kelsey. Will you be my mate?" His wards' terminology slipped out, and although the words felt right to him, Jase wanted no misunderstandings. "Will you marry me?"

Geneva pulled back and studied him carefully. "And just who will I be marrying?"

"Jase Guardian. And Jason Merrick."

"Both of you." To his amazement, she actually seemed to approve. But he felt the need to explain, anyway.

"I can't go back to who I was, Geneva, any more than I can give up what I've become. Do you think you can live with the two halves of me?"

She smiled and moved back into his arms again. "I'll have the best of both worlds."

Still Jase refused to believe it would be so easy. "I'm warning you, Geneva. You'll also have to live with the worst from both worlds."

"I've managed all right so far, wouldn't you say?" The adoration in her eyes took his breath away even before she actually said the words. "I love you so very much, Jase. We'll be fine. Just fine."

Just fine. Such silly, trite, ridiculous little words. Such a foolish statement. But again, it was a start.

And for the man from The Sanctuary, it was more than enough.

Epilogue

"Audrey Merrick, you get out of that water right now!" Geneva shouted out over the lagoon.

Jase watched as his young daughter giggled from the back of Susie, the prehistoric Archelon. Audrey's naked bottom wiggled with glee as she and the huge turtle she was riding once again avoided Geneva and headed out toward deeper water.

On the beach, Geneva planted her hands on her hips and scowled. Jase couldn't help laughing. His angry wife whirled around toward him.

"Make her come in, Jase!" Geneva demanded. "You know I can't swim fast enough to catch her now." Her arm protectively circled the lush, ample curves of her very pregnant belly.

Jase smiled, his eyes feasting on the sight of his wife. She hadn't aged a day since he'd taken her through the barriers and made her his own. *If anything, she's more beautiful than ever,* he thought to himself. But he knew better than to approach Geneva when she was in such a temper. A defiant, spirited toddler and a due date four weeks away didn't always mix very well, especially so late in the day.

"Let Audrey play, sweetheart. You know she loves her wards."

"She's tired. Jase, she's only three years old!"

"I know." Jase fondly turned toward the black-haired, bronze-skinned child. "Youngest guardian in the history of The Sanctuary," he said with a father's pride.

"I don't care! Turtles or no turtles, she needs to go to bed! And unlike Audrey, I can't talk to turtles! So you had better get them both in to shore or else," she warned.

"All right, my love," Jase said, giving in gracefully. He might rule The Sanctuary, but Geneva's word was law when it came to Audrey. "Just five more minutes, I promise."

Some of the frown left Geneva's face, and Jase immediately took advantage. He rose from his spot on the warm sand and encircled her ripe belly with his arms from behind.

"I'm tired of you men always ganging up on me," Geneva grumbled, although Jase felt her relax against his chest, the loose sarong she wore whispering against his skin.

"Thomas and Shawn are just as bad." She gestured out toward the water where the two other guardians were checking on their wards. "Between that incorrigible pair and their dolphins, Audrey's *never* going to wear out a pair of shoes. I don't know who's worse, our brothers or our daughter!"

Jase kissed her neck and turned her exquisite, gravid body around in his arms so he could face her. "I thought you loved dolphins."

"Of course I do! I love *all* animals, but as only the

men on this island can talk to them, I'm at a disadvantage," she said.

A look suddenly crossed Jase's face, and Geneva immediately pounced on it.

"What?" she asked suspiciously.

Jase didn't bother trying to hide anything from her. His secretive nature had disappeared a long time ago, erased by his wife's love.

"About what you just said..." Jase cleared his throat. "It's not exactly correct."

Geneva stared at him in confusion, then her eyes narrowed with sudden comprehension. "Jason Merrick, don't tell me that Audrey is talking to dolphins!"

Jase nodded. "And porpoises. And whales. And—" He hesitated, then blurted it out. "Crocodiles."

Geneva's voice rose two whole octaves. "Do you mean to tell me our three-year-old *baby* is cavorting with *crocodiles?*"

"I'm afraid so."

"And just *when* were you going to tell—"

He kissed her quickly to stop her next torrent of words, for Geneva was fiercely protective of both their daughter and their unborn child. "Look at it this way, Geneva. They know she's a guardian, so she'll be perfectly safe among them."

"Oh, Jase," Geneva wailed. Suddenly she slumped against him. "The four of you are going to drive me to drink." But there was love in her eyes, even as there was love in her voice.

Jase smiled, hugged her tighter against him and savored the moment. His eyes swept across the lagoon to the other members of his family. Both Thomas and Shawn had come so very far in the four years since his marriage to Geneva. And so had he.

Geneva's love had miraculously wiped away the ghosts of the past. Shawn's cure had given Jase the courage to begin his work again in the real world, while Thomas had gradually become his right arm in The Sanctuary.

When little Audrey had been born, Jase thought he'd died and gone to heaven. But Geneva remained his heart and soul. With her help, The Sanctuary had prospered. And with his help, her world had also prospered, for Geneva had found more Steller's sea cows. Geneva's Alaskan Sirenian Institute promised the same high hopes for propagation of the rare species as did The Sanctuary.

And now she would soon grace their lives with another child. Never in his wildest dreams did Jase think life could be so good.

"If this boy I'm carrying is as predisposed to multiple species as Audrey is, I swear, Jase, no more children! I can't sleep nights worrying about the one I have now." Geneva suddenly gasped. "What if this baby's predisposed to *sharks?*"

She shivered in horror, and despite himself Jason laughed.

"Geneva, my love, no sea creature will harm one hair on our children's heads. I give you my word as Senior Guardian." He gently kneaded her aching back. "You look tired. Want to go lie down?"

"I want *Audrey* to go lie down," she insisted, but her body betrayed her. Under his touch the irritation left her face, to be replaced by a yearning passion that still had the ability to make him catch his breath with delicious anticipation.

"A few more minutes outside won't hurt her," Jase

whispered. "We still have a whole half hour of light, and Audrey's uncles will take good care of her."

Geneva looked out toward the water with one last worried expression. "Are you sure, Jase?" she asked, even as she allowed him to lead her up to the bungalow.

"Oh, yes, my Sweet Survivor." He stopped to kiss her, his lips lingering over hers, his eyes full of love as he remembered her words from so long ago.

Everything will be just fine.

Uncover the truth behind

CODE NAME: DANGER

in **Merline Lovelace's** thrilling duo

DANGEROUS TO HOLD

When tricky situations need a cool head, quick wits and a touch of ruthlessness, Adam Ridgeway, director of the top secret OMEGA agency, sends in his team. Lately, though, his agents have had romantic troubles of their own....

NIGHT OF THE JAGUAR
&
THE COWBOY AND THE COSSACK

And don't miss
HOT AS ICE (IM #1129, 2/02)
which features the newest OMEGA adventure!

DANGEROUS TO HOLD is available this February
at your local retail outlet!

Look for ***DANGEROUS TO KNOW,*** the second set of
stories in this collection, in July 2002.

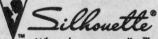
Where love comes alive™

magazine

♥──────────────────────────── **quizzes**

Is he the one? What kind of lover are you? Visit the **Quizzes** area to find out!

♥──────────────────── **recipes for romance**

Get scrumptious meal ideas with our **Recipes for Romance**.

♥───────────────────────── **romantic movies**

Peek at the **Romantic Movies** area to find Top 10 Flicks about First Love, ten Supersexy Movies, and more.

♥──────────────────────────── **royal romance**

Get the latest scoop on your favorite royals in **Royal Romance**.

♥──────────────────────────────────── **games**

Check out the **Games** pages to find a ton of interactive romantic fun!

♥──────────────────────────── **romantic travel**

In need of a romantic rendezvous? Visit the **Romantic Travel** section for articles and guides.

♥──────────────────────────────── **lovescopes**

Are you two compatible? Click your way to the **Lovescopes** area to find out now!

Silhouette® —

where love comes alive—online...

SINTMAG

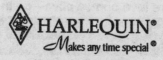